PARANORM WORLD BOOK TWO

A MOON SISTERS NOVEL

JUNE STEVENS WESTERFIELD

THIS book is a work of fiction. Names, characters, places and incidents are the product of the authors' imagination or are used factiously. Any resemblance to actual persons, living or dead, business establishments, events or locales is entirely coincidental.

NO part of this book may be reproduced, scanned, or distributed in any printed or electronic form without permission. Please do not participate in or encourage piracy of copyrighted materials in violation of the author's rights. Purchase only authorized editions.

Immortal Moon
Copyright ©2015 June Stevens Westerfield
All rights reserved.

ISBN: 978-1-63422-152-8
Cover Design by: Marya Heiman
Typography by: Courtney Nuckels
Editing by: Cynthia Shepp

To Patricia. Thank you for raising such a wonderful son so that I could marry him and get you as my second mom.

ONE
Anya

*I*SIDESTEPPED THE FIST COMING AT MY HEAD AND MY opponent pitched forward, his balance off. Taking advantage of the situation, I slammed my fist into his flabby gut. As he doubled over, he reached up and grabbed my thick, red ponytail, yanking me backwards.

Why was it always the hair? It never failed. It didn't matter how big, buff, or macho the guy was, he always went for the hair. Biting my lip, I turned so my back was to him and let him pull me until I could feel his hot, rank breath on my neck. Lifting my knee, I kicked back as hard as I could. My aim was just right, and my foot connected with soft flesh. It was a low blow, but then, so was hair pulling.

"Gah!" the sailor cried out, releasing my hair. I turned to see him fall to his knees, both hands cupping his nether region. I finished him off with a foot to the shoulder, sending him sprawling on his back. The small crowd around the makeshift ring cheered so loud they drowned the ref calling out the ten-count. I stood back, catching my breath. The ref was halfway through the count when the sailor flipped onto his stomach, and then rose to his knees. By the time the count reached nine, the sailor was on both feet, if stumbling a bit.

Damn! That kick to his groin should have put him out. The ref stopped counting, and the fight was back on.

I watched him, warily taking in every movement as he turned and glared at me. His face was bright red, rage radiating from him. *Great.* I pissed him off, and now I had a three-hundred-pound rage monster to contend with. The thought was barely complete when he charged at me, letting out a gruff, angry growl. With my back at the edge of the ring and the sailor's arms outstretched on either side, there was nowhere for me to go to get out of his way. I did the only thing I could. I started running towards him. At the very last moment before our bodies collided, I dropped low and to the side. At the same time, I stretched out my left leg, catching the sailor just above the ankle. He stumbled, his momentum sending his entire body airborne. For one long second, he flew through the air, and then came crashing down face-first several feet away.

Pushing to my feet, I turned to see the sailor rise up to his knees, and then to his feet. *Geezus*, what would it take to put this guy down? Taking a deep breath, I readied myself for another round. The big man took one step forward, swayed, and crumpled to the ground. The crowd went silent, as if they were all holding their breath, while the ref started his count. The sailor didn't attempt to get up again. He just laid there, his chest heaving with the force of his breath, and emitted an occasional moan.

"Ten," announced the ref, and the crowd gave an ear-splitting roar.

"Once again the winner is The Spitfire!" The ref, a tall, lanky man in faded hemp-cloth overalls, grabbed my right wrist and thrust my hand high into the air. The applause doubled.

I tried not to grimace as I nodded to the crowd, which was expected. Extracting myself from the ref's grasp, I quickly stepped over the thick rope that was looped around the center of the warehouse to create a boxing ring. Ignoring the glare of the sailor and the two guys helping him up, I strode directly to the large, dark-skinned man lounging on shipping pallets stacked against the wall near the open bay doors. "Pete, would you tell Slim to quit calling me The Spitfire?"

"Aww hell, Anya, the crowd loves it," Pete drawled. "When the patrons are happy, they bet more, and betting against a skinny, redheaded girl called "The Spitfire" makes them happy. Very, very happy." He waved a small, leather bag stuffed full of coins in the air before tossing it to me.

I caught it easily and pulled open the drawstring to peer inside. "Eighty bucks. That's a damned good take for two fights."

Pete grunted. "Yep. But, damn it, Anya, do you have to take them down so damned fast? You gotta give the people a show. They keep betting against you because you're going up against the biggest dudes I can find, but what they really want is a performance. If you keep dropping them in the first three minutes, the bets are gonna stop rolling in. I got a business to run here."

"Yeah, I know, I know, it's all about the entertainment." I rolled my eyes. It wasn't the first time Pete had given me this lecture. "Hell, Pete, I can't help it if you keep recruiting buffoons that don't know how to fight."

Pete's Fight House was located on the riverfront for one major reason; it attracted big, burly sailors wanting to test their skills against other dudes and win a little money in the process. The bigger the guys fighting, the larger the crowds and bets they drew. When I was fighting, the crowd was always huge. It didn't matter that I was undefeated; there was always a multitude of people willing to bet against me. The larger my opponent, the bigger the bets. But size didn't matter as much as fighting skill. It wasn't bragging to say I had skills in spades. I'd trained at the Academy with the City Guard recruits, and until she'd moved out a few months ago, I'd sparred daily with my sister Fiona, one of the best combat mages the Black Blade Guard had to offer. I knew what I was doing in a fight. And with few exceptions, the big guys Pete recruited rarely had any real fighting skills.

Pete snorted. "I can't be testing their skills before I slate fights. The biggest dudes get pitted against you. It's what people want to see. It's up to you to make it more entertaining."

"Okay, I'll try harder next time." I laughed. It was pretty much how this conversation ended every time we had it, which was weekly. "Okay, I gotta dash. I'll catch you next week, Pete."

"Sure thing, Anya," Pete said, and then pulled his attention to the next fight already taking place in the ring.

I grabbed my hat, cloak, and bag from the shelf Pete kept in the corner for fighters' belongings. Slipping my canvas shopping bag over my shoulder and across my chest, I was just about to step out the door into the late morning sun when I heard a hoarse cry behind me.

"Cheat!"

I turned to see the sailor I'd just beaten, his face scraped and bloody, hobbling towards me with the help of his two friends.

"She's a paranorm. No norm girl could move like that," his friend, a tall blond wearing heavy denim pants and a grungy shirt of indeterminable color, called out.

The companion on the other side of the sailor was short and broad. His hair was a couple of shades darker than the blond man, but he wore clothes that, except for the shirt's color, were identical to the sailor and the blond. Pretty generic clothing for sailors. His face twisted in anger. "We've been cheated."

Oh, shit balls, this wasn't good.

The standard rules for fighting houses and street-fighting leagues was that anyone could attend the fights, anyone could bet, but only norms could fight in norm-slated matches. It kept the playing field level. Vamps and Shifters had super strength and speed that gave them unfair advantages that norms couldn't compete with. Some houses allowed mages to compete in norm fights because although they could use their powers for an advantage, most didn't. It cut down on accusations of cheating. Of course, there were fight-house owners and bookies that had paranorms on their payroll. They were put into fights as norms to hustle, but Pete ran a clean establishment. Pete's fights were all above board, and he hated being accused of allowing cheating in his club. *Really* hated it.

Before I could react in any way, Pete stood, his considerable mass sliding off the crate with the grace of a cat. I couldn't help but grin as the three guys stopped, their eyes taking him in. When seated, his affable grin splitting his face, Pete looked as cute and cuddly as a child's teddy bear, but when he stood, he looked more like a grizzly. It was easy to mistake the girth under his gray denim overalls as flab. But his six-foot frame was packed with solid muscle.

"I can assure you, gentlemen," he said in his thick, jovial voice, "Anya is not a paranorm. She is just a good fighter."

"Bullshit," the sailor grunted, holding one arm across his ribs. I wondered if perhaps one or two had been cracked. "There is no way she's norm. She's too fast, too strong."

"Yeah," his blond buddy chimed in, obviously bolstered by the fact that there were three of them against Pete. "Look at how pale she is. And she has that cloak even though it's plenty warm out. And why does she need a wide-brimmed hat? She's got to be a vampire."

That was their evidence? *Oh, please.* Though it was just mid-morning, it was shaping up to be a warm spring day, but it had been cool when I left home at dawn. Granted, I did wear the hat to protect my skin, but it was because the creamy, white skin tone that came with coppery red hair burned easily, and I hated freckles. But no way was I going to explain any of that to those boneheads. Instead, I grabbed my hat in one hand, the cloak in the other and, holding them out to either side of my body, took several steps backward until I was out of the building and standing full in the sun. I turned my face up towards the sky.

Vampires were allergic to the UV rays in sunlight. It was a side effect of the N-V virus that caused vampirism. Though I burned easily, a few minutes out in the sun wouldn't make a difference, but a vampire's skin would start turning pink after several seconds, then red within minutes. The longer the exposure, the worse the reaction. After an hour of direct exposure, most vampires would have third degree burns on the exposed area. A vampire would never step full into the sun, even if their allergy was relatively mild. Most didn't go out between sunrise and sunset at all if they could help it. I'd only met one vampire who didn't seem to have a reaction to the sun, but even he wore a wide hat and cloak if he went out during the day.

After a full minute, I looked back at the trio still standing next to Pete. He was grinning, and the guys all had murderous looks on their faces. I smiled sweetly, trying to not let it be a smirk. "See, not a vamp."

"Then you are a shifter or a mage, you bitch," the

sailor growled at me, his eyes blazing.

"Whoa, fella," Pete drawled. "There will be no name calling in my house. Just calm down."

"Don't tell us to calm down," the dark-haired friend spat. "She's a fraud, and you allowed it. You hustled us."

That was not the best thing he could say to Pete. I almost felt sorry for them.

Pete gave a barely perceptible nod and three beefy men came to stand behind the sailor and his buddies. "I think we should go to my office and discuss your allegations," Pete said, his tone low and deceptively polite.

I slapped the straw hat on my head, wiggled my fingers at the scared-looking trio, and hightailed it out of there. I didn't want to see what happened if the three guys put up a fuss.

Once I was around the corner and out of sight, I started running. Pete would keep the three occupied for a while, but I didn't want to be nearby when they left the fight house. They wouldn't be in a good mood.

I jogged away from the docks, weaving through the narrow alleys between warehouses and fish stands, towards my ultimate destination. I was on my way to the Public Market this morning when I got sidetracked at Pete's, as I so often did.

I stopped running when I reached the edge of the

lot outside the main market building. On any given day, it would be easy to blend in with groups of shoppers that browsed the maze of lean-tos and shacks housing blacksmiths, weavers, and other craftsmen. But today wasn't just any day. It was mid-week during the one week a month that merchants and farmers traveled from all over Appalachia to Nash City to sell their wares. Families also traveled from hundreds of miles around to shop during market week. The lot teemed with shoppers and merchants. I knew it would be just as crowded inside the huge building that had been a sports stadium before the Cataclysm. Even if the three sailors did come looking for me, they would have a heck of a time finding me.

Just in case, though, I rolled up my cloak and stuck it in my canvas shopping bag. I did the same with the straw hat. I really did need something to protect my skin from the bright sun, but I'd made eighty bucks off the match with the sailor. I could spring for a new hat quite easily. I pulled out the ribbon holding my hair and ran my fingers through the silky copper strands falling about my shoulders. The back of my head still smarted from my hair being pulled.

Satisfied the sailor and his buddies wouldn't automatically pick me out in a crowd with my hair down, I headed into the market building. My first stop was my sister's booth.

"Hey, Rivs, what's shakin'?" I called as I approached.

River turned from the bin where she was arranging a pile of tomatoes she'd grown in her rooftop garden, flashing her brilliant smile at me. The smile quickly faded into a look of motherly concern. "Anya, where is your hat? You're going to freckle!"

I found her admonishment comical, considering she spent 90% of her time out in the sun tending her plants or working at her market booth, yet she rarely wore sun protection of any kind. Her skin was as pale as mine, paler actually. Paired with her white-blonde hair, it made her look fragile, almost ethereal. Yet she never burned or freckled.

"Geez, Rivs, don't nag. It's in my bag. I was thinking about buying a new hat today."

She eyed me suspiciously. "I expected you earlier. You've been over at Pete's, haven't you?"

"Yeah," I said, grabbing an apple out of a bin and taking a bite. If it had been anyone else in my family, I might have thought about lying, or at least giving them a smart-assed remark, but not River. Despite her eternal motherliness, she never nagged me about street-fighting. She seemed to understand it was something I needed to do, even if neither of us really understood why. When I came home with bruises or cuts, she just cooed and soothed and gave me potions or poultices to get better.

"So, I'm guessing one or more of your opponents didn't take too well to being beaten by a little girl."

"I'm not a little girl," I huffed. "I'm three inches taller than you."

She grinned. "You're a little girl to those beefy blockheads you fight. I'm guessing you are hiding out in the crowd until they disperse."

Oh, how well she knew me. "You know I already planned to come shopping this morning. And with the loot I made at the fight, I have an excuse to spend a little extra time looking at pretties."

"Whatever you say," she said, laughing. "Just don't stay out too long. If you're tired tonight at work, Pinky will know you've been fighting again, and he'll be a grumpy pants for days."

"No worries, Rivs. I'll browse around a bit and get home in time to get plenty of beauty rest before my shift tonight." I gave her a light kiss on the forehead. "See you later."

She went back to her stall to help the crowd of customers perusing her herbs and vegetables.

"And don't forget to buy a new hat!" I heard her call as I headed down the aisle towards my favorite clothing stall.

Two
Anya

An hour later, I had two cute and sexy tops, a corset, several yards of fabric for new skirts, and a new cloth shopping bag to carry them in since my other bag was full with my cloak and hat. I also had a new wool hat with a wide floppy brim pulled down on my head so just a bit of my hair was visible. I had gone a little overboard and only had a couple of bucks from my winnings left. But, I hadn't touched the money I'd brought to shop with, so I figured I'd actually been quite restrained.

It was nearly noon. After grabbing a fish taco at a food stall near the bridge, I headed across the river to the pub where I lived with River and our adoptive father, Pinky.

Just as I reached the highest part of Foot Bridge, the only pre-Cataclysm bridge still crossing the Cumberland River, a gust of wind blew my new hat from my head. The long, braided-leather cord kept it from flying away. Instead, it flopped against my back. I didn't bother trying to put it back on, since I was well away from the market and heading home. Besides, I was sure the sailors had given up and gone back to their boat.

About halfway across the bridge, I heard a shout and the pounding of feet behind me. I turned to look, wondering if perhaps a traveler had mistakenly brought a horse- or oxen-driven wagon onto the pedestrian-only bridge. No such luck. The sailor I'd given a beatdown to earlier at Pete's and his two buddies were several yards behind me, but moving in fast. They pushed other walkers aside as they made their way towards me. Damn, so they hadn't gone back to their boat.

A small knot of fear formed in my stomach. There were three of them and one of me. While I was confident I could whip any one of them with no problem, I certainly wasn't vain or stupid enough to think I could take on all three. I did the only thing I could do. I ran.

As I raced down the bridge, weaving in and out of other pedestrians, I went over my options. I was about a mile from home. I had worked all night, and instead of going to bed, I'd gone down to the waterfront to fight at Pete's. My normal energy was starting to wane. There was no way I would make it all the way home without them catching me. They were chasing me in broad daylight across a crowded bridge. I had no doubt they would attack me in public too. Just getting to a busier street was not going to work. I glanced over at the wide cart-and-wagon bridge that paralleled Foot Bridge. It was several feet lower than Foot Bridge and rickshaws, surreys, riders on horseback, and large industrial wagons pulled by oxen lumbered across it. I could jump down, and if I managed not to break an ankle or my neck, or get run over by a vehicle, I still would only be a few seconds ahead of the thugs once I exited the bridge. Possibly with even less of a lead, given the time it would take to jump, recover, and start running again.

Nearing the end of the bridge, I frantically searched for another solution. Of course there wasn't a City Guard around when I needed one. The buildings of Old Nash loomed ahead of me. My only option was to get off the open street and into the Slums as quickly as possible. I knew this area like the back of my hand, and I was pretty sure the three following me didn't. I could lose them by weaving in and out of alleyways and crevices between the old pre-Cataclysm buildings and the shacks that were built in every open spot between them. That was back when the world had raged and burned, and tens of thousands of refugees had crammed inside the city walls to survive.

The bridge stretched across the river and a little bit over dry land. I spied the small opening in the railing, the only announcement of the staircase leading down to the street below. There was a narrow alley between the building below and the bridge, so I would have to be fast and not get caught in it. On the other side of the bridge was one of the derelict buildings that made up the largest part of the slums. Once a sleek business building constructed mostly of glass, it was now where some of the poorest inhabitants of Nash, mostly Norms like me, lived. I shuddered involuntarily, as I always did, at the thought of living in that sad, dilapidated place. The glass was long gone and the bottom windows were covered with boards, tarps, and blankets to protect the inhabitants from the weather. A few of the upper floors, occupied by vampires that didn't mind walking ten or fifteen flights of stairs, were also covered. Most of the building had gaping holes where floor-to-ceiling glass walls had once been.

I had friends living in that building, some of the regulars at Pete's and other fight houses around the city. If I could just get inside, I could lose the sailors in the maze of make-shift halls and rooms. If you didn't know how to navigate it, you could get very lost, and the people that lived there didn't take kindly to having strangers tromp through their home. I could easily find my way through to the doors on the other side of the building, and no one would think twice about my presence. I shouldn't have any problems, but the sailors would be slowed down.

Only a few blocks from home, going into the building would take me in the opposite direction, but it seemed to be my best bet for losing the thugs. My decision made, I veered to the right, barely missing a woman pushing a baby carriage, and headed for the stairs. I heard a shout behind me and knew the sailors had seen me. I jumped down the crumbling steps two at a time. When I reached the bottom, I veered right again, this time to pass under the bridge.

I had taken about three steps away from the stairs, when a large hand clamped down over my mouth. Simultaneously, an arm snaked around my waist. I was pulled tight against a hard, muscled body. Terror seized me. I tried to scream, but only managed a muffled grunt. I clawed at the hands that held me and kicked my feet furiously, but nothing seemed to work against my captor.

I felt hot breath against my ear. "Calm down, Ginger. I'm not going to hurt you."

Even if I hadn't recognized the voice that whispered in my ear, only one person in my life had ever called me Ginger. I stopped struggling and let myself be pulled into the shadowed recess under the bridge. Within seconds, I found myself sandwiched between the hard concrete wall of the alcove under the bridge and the just as hard body of a six-and-a-half-foot-tall vampire. I put my hands between us, but he quickly pulled them away and pressed closer. His long, dark cloak fell around us, so that it was completely shielding me from view.

I opened my mouth, but before I could speak, or even figure out what I was going to say, he hissed in my ear, "Shh. They won't be able to see us, just be quiet."

I clamped my mouth shut, and then followed suit with my eyes, since all I could see was a black shirt covered chest. It was a struggle to keep my breath steady and quiet. I was winded from the run, and there was little air under the cloak. With each breath, I inhaled the scent of the man pressed against me. The air grew hotter and thicker by the moment, or maybe it was just my blood. My pulse raced and my skin tingled in ways that had nothing to do with the dangerous thugs pursuing me, and everything to do with the dangerous man protecting me.

Heavy thudding sounded on the stairs.

"Where did she go?" a gruff voice shouted just a few feet behind Jarrett.

The breath caught in my throat. They were ten or so feet away from us. How could they not see us? My body stiffened, waiting, expecting one of them to spy us. Clenching my fists, I prepared for battle. I wasn't afraid of them with Jarrett there to have my back. One against three was suicide, but two against three, especially when one of the two was a bad-ass vampire, were more even odds. Except, I was exhausted and wasn't sure just how long I would last. The only thing in my favor was that the sailor I had beaten earlier had to be as tired and achy as I was.

When the next shout came, it wasn't to reveal our poor hiding skills.

"Come on," one of the sailors called from a little farther away. "I think she went into that building. Stupid little bitch."

Jarrett's arms tightened around me, holding me still when I would have stepped around him to show that meat-head what a stupid little bitch could do when she was pissed off. Running footsteps sounded then faded away.

Jarrett stepped back. "They're gone. We should get out of here in case they decide to double back."

I tried to ignore the fact that I suddenly felt cold and bereft without his arms around me, despite the warmth of the day. "What are you doing here? How did you know I was in trouble? Why didn't they see us?" The questions came out in rapid fire succession, not giving him time to answer.

He laughed. "I'll answer your twenty questions as I walk you home."

Bristling, my independent streak reared its ugly head, but I tamped it down. I was tempted to tell him I was capable of taking care of myself, but the truth was, it would be wise to have the backup just in case the three thugs were smarter than I thought. Besides, spending a few minutes with Jarrett Campbell would be no hardship. My eyes scraped over his tall, muscular frame. Heat suffused my body as the memory of the last time I'd been caught between that body and a wall flitted through my mind. I shook my head slightly to clear it.

"We should get going, then." I hurried up the narrow path between a red brick building and the concrete wall of the bridge ramp with Jarrett on my heels. When we reached the next street over, Jarrett grabbed my arm and pulled me behind him as he surveyed the street. We were only a few feet away from the second entrance to the slum building the sailors had gone into. If they came out now, we would be in plain sight. But they were nowhere to be seen. They were either searching the upper floors or had been chased out the other side.

"Looks like the coast is clear. I don't want to take any chances, though. Let's get out of here." Before he finished the sentence, Jarrett's hand slid down my arm to capture my hand. He started across the street, pulling me behind him. We quickly weaved in and out of the traffic of rickshaws and ox-carts. On the other side of the street, our pace didn't slow until we slid into an alleyway, putting an entire building between us and the line of sight of anyone near the bridge.

"So, why did those guys want to rip your head off? I'm guessing it had something to do with street fighting," he said casually, once we'd settled into a slow, comfortable pace, our joined hands swinging between us.

"Of course not," I said with mock indigence. "It was a reputable fight house."

Jarrett let out a low, throaty laugh that sent shivers of awareness vibrating through me. "Of course it was. I thought you promised Fiona you would stop fighting."

"I promise her that on a weekly basis, neither of us really expects me to live up to it," I told him, turning my face up and giving him what I hoped was my most devilish grin. "Besides, what I promised was to stop fighting guys juiced up on shifter blood. Though, really, that guy was so blundering and graceless, I don't think a blast of manic super strength would have helped him win. It would have just made him more of an asshole about losing."

Jarrett laughed again, grinning down at me from beneath the wide brim of his hat. "Considering he and his buddies are currently hunting you with murder on their minds, I don't think he needed any help in the asshole department."

"True enough."

I turned down a darker, narrower alley, pulling Jarrett with me via our still joined hands. We weren't far from the pub I called home, but this way would take longer to get there. Instead of taking the direct route and going a couple of blocks up then a couple more over on the main thoroughfares, we would have to weave through alleys and walkways created by the rough-built shacks that filled the spaces between older buildings, turning what had once been streets and parking lots into homes for poor, mainly norm, families.

"Do you know where you're going?" Jarrett asked.

"I've been roaming these streets since I was a kid. I know my way around."

"Okay," he said simply, following me as we walked single-file between two buildings.

The narrow walkway opened to a wider street lined by small, single story dwellings that had been built during the cataclysm. They were now home to the poorest of Nash City's citizens. The residents of the Slums were generally norms or mages with very little magical abilities. They were the lowest class, people who couldn't perform magic and had to take the least paying, most menial jobs. As a norm, if it weren't for Pinky and my permanent job at the pub, I would probably live in a tiny shack somewhere, if I'd even survived to adulthood.

I quickly pushed all thoughts of my childhood and lack of paranormal abilities out of my head and focused on the man that was once again walking by my side. "Okay, it's my turn to ask questions."

He gave my hand a little squeeze. "Go ahead, I'm an open book."

Ha! That was a crock. The tall, sexy vampire was a walking enigma. About six months ago, we'd spent a couple of weeks together in close proximity. He'd been acting as my bodyguard while he and my sister worked a case. My family had been potential targets. We'd had several long talks, as well as other intimate communications, yet I barely knew him beyond a few random facts. Even if I had a hundred years, I didn't think I'd uncover all there was to know about Jarrett Campbell. I would just have to do with the most pressing questions. "How did you come to be under that bridge exactly when I needed you?"

"I'm Batman," he said in a deep, husky whisper.

"You're a what-man?"

He laughed that sexy laugh that made my whole body go tingly. "Sorry, bad pre-cataclysm joke. I was down by the docks. I'd just gotten to town and was stepping off the boat when I heard shouting. I looked up and saw fiery hair, and since I haven't seen anyone else with that particular shade of red, I guessed it was you. You didn't seem to want to talk to those fine gentlemen, so I figured you would take the first exit you could off the bridge. I run faster than you, so there I was, just in time to save the damsel in distress."

He flashed a wide, boyish grin.

Rolling my eyes, I pretended to ignore the remark. I would have said something snippy about not needing to be saved, but I kinda had. "And how come they didn't see us?"

"It's my super power. I told you I was Batman. Well, technically Batman didn't have any super powers. He was just a rich guy with lots of gadgets. So I guess I'm Superman."

I stopped in the middle of the street, our joined hands pulling him to a stop as well. I couldn't help the baffled laughter that rolled out of me. "What in the crap are you talking about? Do you have some sort of Vampire dementia? You've probably been out in the sun too long."

"Are you telling me Pinky never told you stories about superheroes? I mean, sure, there haven't been any comic books around for a couple hundred years, but I would have thought Pinky would have been a fan since he was a teenager when the best comics were created. Not to mention the amazing movies." He flashed me a genuinely puzzled look. "Captain America,

Spiderman, Guardians of the Galaxy. He never told you about those?"

I shook my head, still laughing at his look of indignation. "Sorry, no. As kids, my sisters and I spent a lot of time at the City Library. Carly is like our honorary aunt. She watched us while Pinky slept mornings after working all night. I've read a lot of books, but I've never heard of comic books or super heroes."

He gave a long, put-upon sigh as we started walking again. "That is truly tragic. I can't even begin to try and educate you on the wonders you have missed."

"Well, then I guess you'll just have to tell me the real reason those thugs couldn't see us."

"If I must," he said in mock defeat. "It really is my power though. I can bend light energy around me—and one or two additional people if we are close and touching—to appear invisible for a short time."

He dropped my hand, the air shimmered around him, and he faded from sight.

"Wow, that's a pretty cool power to have," I said, rubbing my hand that now felt cold without his touch.

He faded back into view. "Yeah, it can come in handy."

A thought popped into my head as we started walking again. "That's why you aren't rushing to get out of the sun. I wondered why you never seemed very concerned about the sunlight. I thought maybe you just didn't have the same allergy as other vampires."

"No, I have the allergy, or at least I think I do. It took me a while to realize it, but along with the light bending, I have this natural energy force field around me. I don't have to consciously think about it like I do for invisibility, it's just there."

"Were you a mage before you were changed?" I was genuinely curious about Jarrett and hoped he wouldn't think I was being rude.

"Nope. Not even a little. I had no idea magic, vampires, or any of that existed. I spent my life in the sun, though, and I think that is part of why my powers manifested the way they did."

I nodded. I knew that even norms usually developed some sort of magical abilities when they became vampires. The ability to manipulate energy came from brain's activity level. Norms used around 10-15% usually. Level one mages registered at least 25% brain activity. The N-V virus that caused vampirism often activated more areas in the victim's brain, giving norms some magical abilities and increasing those of a mage. Though there wasn't any real proof of why different abilities manifested in different people, it was speculated that it had to do with the brain areas that were active. In a class at the Academy, I remember reading that some mage scientist put forth that the powers a person would have after being infected with

N-V virus could be loosely predicted by their personality and natural abilities.

That made me curious about why Jarrett had spent so much time in the sun before he was made, but before I could ask, he stopped walking. I realized we were standing in the alley behind the pub, right in front of the back door.

"Here you are, home. Safe and sound."

"So I am," I said, trying not to show my disappointment at not getting to ask the questions bustling around in my brain. "I'd offer you a drink as payment for helping me escape those thugs, but it's already after noon and I need to get some sleep if I'm going to be worth anything at work tonight. Rain check?"

"I'm not sure how long I'll be in the city. I probably won't be able to cash in a rain check."

"Oh," I said, trying harder this time not to show my disappointment that I wouldn't get to see him again any time soon.

I reached for the door handle, determined to make a graceful exit, when he took a step closer to me. Before I could process what was happening, he had one hand wrapped in my hair, gently pulling my head back, and the other around my waist, pulling me tight against him.

"I'll take my reward now," he said, a fraction of a

second before his mouth came down on mine. The kiss started hot and quickly proceeded to scorching as I automatically opened to him and kissed him back with a hunger I hadn't known existed. He tasted so exotic, yet achingly familiar. The alley melted away as hot tremors slid through me. There was something about this man that decimated my brain and made me abandon what little sense of propriety I had to start with. Just as I was sinking into the kiss, my hands grasping at his shoulders like a life raft, he pulled away from me.

When I looked up at him, I could see the fire in his eyes. He was as turned on as I was, I knew it. But then he popped out his cocky, boyish grin and said, "Sweet dreams, Ginger. Later."

Before I could speak or throw a rock at him, he was at the end of the block and disappeared around a corner. I leaned against the door, silently cursing Jarrett, and wondering if my jelly legs would make it upstairs to my bed.

Three
Jarrett

KISSING ANYA MOON HAD BEEN THE WRONG thing to do. Saving her had been the right thing to do. She was, after all, his best friend's sister. The fact that he'd wanted to rip to shreds the three assholes who had dared to chase her and feed them to the fish in the river had everything to do with protecting his friend, and nothing to do with the strange possessiveness gripping him the moment he'd recognized her as she'd ran across the bridge.

Yep. And his name was Princess Moonbeam.

Kissing Anya Moon had been the wrong thing to do because it had brought the memory of her taste and feel to the forefront of his mind when he thought he'd put their brief encounter behind him. She had lingered in his thoughts and dreams over the past six months like no other woman ever had, and just when she'd faded from his daily thoughts, there she was again. But mostly, kissing Anya Moon had been the wrong thing to do because now he wanted nothing more than to go back and kiss her again and again and again.

Jarrett groaned to himself and stomped up the stairs of the Nash City Black Blade Guard headquarters building to the twenty-fifth floor where he inserted a crystal into a slot next to the door to unlock it and entered the hallway where his private room was located. He strode to the last door and repeated the crystal procedure to enter the large room that served as his private office and, when he didn't have other options, his sleeping quarters whenever he was in Nash City. He rarely used the room since he was rarely in the city, but he kept a few items of clothing and some spare weapons in the room, just in case. He mostly used it for the reason he'd come here today—to contact his commander in Atlanta with the private scry-crystal.

It was times like this that he sorely missed the cell phone age. Even with the privacy vulnerabilities of technology, with a little added magic, it had been a simple task to get a secure line to his commander from anywhere in the world. While portable scry-crystals had taken up some of the slack after the Cataclysm, they could only be used to contact other scry-crystals within a couple hundred-mile radius and they were impossible to secure. When it was time to report in to Atlanta, Jarrett had to go to the nearest allied city-state with a Black Blade Guard headquarters building. Each one had a network of large scry-crystals tuned exclusively to other headquarters. In Nash, he had a large, wall-mounted crystal in his room that was coded to connect with only one other crystal, the one in the office of the Kukri division commander in Atlanta. The crystal was protected with privacy spells and kept at full power by Blade chargers.

Sitting at the desk, he placed his hand on the blank crystal. His personal energy signature activated it, and the clear, glassy surface turned cloudy as the connection to the crystal several hundred miles away was made. After a few seconds, the fog cleared and revealed a vampire who appeared to be in his mid-thirties with close-cropped blond hair and a close-shaven jaw. Commander Hugh Westbrook was relatively new to his position as the leader of the Kukri division. A little over sixty years ago, he replaced Commander Bonassio who had founded the Kukri as a squad of spies and assassins in the early years of the Spanish Inquisition. Over the centuries, the job description had not varied much, though they did a little less assassinating and more tracking and apprehending dangerous paranorm criminals.

"Campbell, good to hear from you. It's been a while, any progress?" Westbrook said, offering a tight smile.

Westbrook was friendly, but direct and to the point. He didn't waste time with idle chitchat. Jarrett appreciated that because he detested these reports. It was the most tedious part of his job, and this particular report was especially loathsome.

"Nothing positive, sir. All substantiated evidence points to the death of Agent Solahan when she fell from the building in Detroit eight months ago," he replied, choosing his words carefully.

"I'm sorry to hear that. Solahan was a fine operative. What is your case recommendation?"

"That we suspend investigation, unless and until further evidence surfaces."

Westbrook nodded solemnly. "With current evidence, I hereby designate Agent Cora Solahan as killed in the line of duty."

Pain and regret sliced through Jarret, but he didn't let it show. "Yes, sir. I will file the appropriate paperwork to close the case and have it sent out with the next messenger." Blade messengers relayed documents and packages between the headquarters of each city-state. Messengers left Nash for Atlanta every other day.

"Very good. Anything else?" Westbrook asked.

"Actually, Commander there is one last thing. I would like to formally request permission to take my mandatory leave," Jarrett asked on impulse.

Westbrook's eyes went wide. He was almost as shocked at the request as Jarrett. "This is the first time in sixty-three years I haven't had to force you to take your mandatory leave. Should I be concerned?"

No, but I think I should be, Jarrett thought. Out loud, he said. "No sir. This has been a difficult assignment and I could use a little time to decompress."

"Understandable. Always hard to lose a fellow agent. Consider yourself on leave as soon as you hand your paperwork over to the messenger. Report back in two weeks to resume duty," the commander said. Then added, "I believe you have some extra time built up, if you need more than two weeks, file a request via scry or certified messenger if you aren't near a Blade headquarters."

"Two weeks will suffice, thank you Sir."

The commander nodded and reached forward to touch his scry-crystal. "Westbrook out," he said, and the crystal went cloudy then blank.

Jarrett let out an exasperated sigh. He'd had zero intentions of requesting leave before he'd seen Anya this morning. The plan had been to conduct his business in Nash, then be headed out of the city, either back to Atlanta or out on another assignment, by tomorrow morning. Now, he had nothing to do and nowhere to be for the next two weeks.

He shook his head and rummaged through his desk drawers to find the report forms he needed to fill out to officially end his current assignment. *Two friggin' weeks.* He wondered what had possessed him to request leave, but he had a feeling he already knew.

Kissing Anya Moon had been the wrong thing to do.

An hour and a half later, Jarrett handed an envelope full of completed forms to the clerk behind the counter in the mailroom of the Blade headquarters. As far as his boss and the Blades were concerned, he was officially on leave the moment the packet left his fingers. But he had one more report to make before he could put this case behind him—if he ever could.

He left the mailroom, used his identity crystal to access the private lift, and rode up to the top floor. Stepping into a hallway, he was welcomed by the sounds of shuffling papers, clicking typewriters, and low voices as support staff for the commander of the Nash City Blades went about their jobs. Jarrett strode past offices of secretaries, typists, researchers, and the highest-ranking Nash City Blades agents and went directly to the large office at the end of the hall. He tapped a single, cursory knock on the door and went in. He was surprised to find the office empty, but a deep, rich laugh made him turn.

Sam Harrison, the Commander General—though he abhorred anyone using his title—of the Nash City division of the Black Blade Guards, was sitting on the edge of a desk with three women surrounding him as he told what the women seemed to think was a funny story. Jarrett chuckled softly to himself. Sam could be reciting a market shopping list, but as long as he flashed those pearly whites and flexed his massive arm and chest muscles, he could hold almost any woman's attention. As Jarrett watched, Sam raised one eyebrow high and the women giggled in unison. Shaking his head, Jarrett turned and went into Sam's office to wait. He knew the man would tire shortly of being fawned over and be back to his all-business self.

Less than five minutes later, Sam strode into the office. "Hey, Buddy, didn't know you were back in town," he said, his words belying the complete lack of surprise in his eyes to see Jarrett.

"Just got in a couple of hours ago," Jarrett said, though he figured Sam already knew that. His friend liked to pretend ignorance, but he tended to know everything that went on in the Blades' building. He might not have known when Jarrett got into town, but odds were Sam had known the moment Jarrett had stepped into the building, or at the very least, the moment he'd first used his ID crystal.

Sam extended a fist and Jarrett met it with his own, bumping his friend's knuckles in greeting. It was a ridiculous gesture they'd mockingly started long ago when it was the "in thing" for guys to do, but somehow it had stuck. Now, centuries later, it was their standard form of greeting.

"On assignment?" Sam asked, settling into the chair behind his desk.

Jarrett shook his head. "Not as of about fifteen minutes ago. I'm officially on mandatory leave."

"And your case?"

"Closed."

Disappointment clouded Sam's dark features. "So no sign of Cora at all?"

"No. There have been whispers and rumors, but I've ran them all down. I haven't laid eyes on her since…"

"The night she jumped," Sam finished for him.

A knot formed in Jarrett's throat. "Yeah."

During the Cataclysm, what had once been the state of Michigan was flooded with water and nuclear radiation. The parts that remained above water created an island in the middle of the Michigan Gulf called Detroit, or No Man's Land to most. The ruins were overrun with criminals, mostly vampires. Detroit was out of bounds to most Blades, the Council of Elders deeming it unsafe for agents. But he wasn't most Blades, he was Kukri, an assassin. Even Kukri only ventured into No Man's Land under the direst of circumstances. To Jarrett, rescuing his former partner had qualified. But as they stood on top of that crumbling building on the edge of a rocky cliff, she hadn't wanted to be saved. Standing on the ledge, she begged him to leave her alone, and then she jumped, disappearing into the churning, rocky waters below.

"Jarrett." Sam's voice pulled Jarrett back to the present.

"What?"

"Where were you man? You just kind of left for a minute," Sam said, his voice tinged with concern.

"Sorry, I have a hard time not playing it over and over in my head. She begged me not to make her go back to the Blades, to let her start over with a new life. And when I told her she had to come back, she jumped."

"It's understandable that you're having a hard time with it. Watching anyone commit suicide is hard to cope with, but when it's a partner and friend—especially one you have a history with like you had with Cora—there is going to be real trauma," Sam said.

Jarrett shook his head. "That's the thing, it just doesn't feel like that. There was just something off about Cora. Her words were sad, desperate even. Yet, in her eyes, it wasn't sadness. It was anger, fury, hatred. She did not look like a woman bent on suicide."

"You think she survived the fall." It was a statement, not a question.

"It's what I've been working the past eight months to prove, but so far nothing. Logic says she hit the rocks, was knocked out, pulled under by the current, and drowned. Even a vampire would die in such violent seas. It was storming, and I'm pretty sure her arm was broken before she jumped. Even if she didn't hit rocks, swimming would have been near impossible."

"But still possible. Even injured she would have been strong and could hold her breath for quite a while. She could have survived."

Jarrett shrugged. "I thought so, too. There was no sign of her body, but I also never saw her swim out, and I watched and searched the shoreline for hours. If she'd been there, I should have seen her. I've followed rumors and possible sightings of a redheaded vampire, but to no avail. Each one was a dead-end."

Sam let out a sigh. "The case is closed now, so you've given up?"

Jarrett shrugged. "I had no choice. It's been eight months. The commander wanted to close the case immediately. It was only my gut feeling that perhaps she survived that allowed me to keep working it this long. The last time I checked in, two months ago, he told me I needed to wrap it up. It has been more than six weeks since I've had any kind of lead. I figured now was time. All I can do is hope that if she's alive, she has found a peaceful, happy life."

"I'm with you in the doubt department," Sam said, shaking his head. "Cora is not—was not—the type of woman to just give up and kill herself. Not even if she was distraught, though it is difficult to imagine Cora hysterical. Do you think she really loved that prick, or maybe she was brainwashed?"

Jarrett thought back to the gang leader Cora had been assigned to kill, but hadn't. He couldn't get the look on her face, or the sound of her screams, out of his head when she'd seen the man's dead body after Jarrett had done the job. "I don't know. She was with him and his gang for nearly two years. Anything could have happened to her."

Sam gave a small, almost imperceptible nod. "Then perhaps it's better not to find her. Maybe she really did just need to get away from the Blades and find some peace."

"Maybe," Jarrett agreed, but he wasn't so sure. "Whatever happened, the case is officially closed."

"And the official report?" Sam asked.

"Agent Cora Solahan of the Black Blade Guard, Kukri Division, died in the line of duty after being held captive in excess of one year by a slaver gang she had been ordered to infiltrate and spy on. Her death occurred during rescue after an intense fight. She ventured too near the ledge, lost her balance, and fell," Jarrett repeated what he'd typed into the report less than an hour before.

"You haven't told anyone your suspicion that she hadn't lost contact with her handler because she was being held captive, but rather because she'd switched sides?"

"Just you. I had no real proof, other than her hysterical rantings on that roof."

Sam raised an eyebrow. "Other than the fact that the fight you mentioned in the report was actually her trying to kill you, not her trying to escape from Dread's men?"

"Details," Jarrett quipped. "You know those reports are supposed to be concise. I was just being efficient."

Sam rolled his eyes, but then nodded. "True. If it matters, I agree with your decision not to give voice to your suspicions. I believe you're correct, and if she truly is gone, sullying her name does nothing. Better to have her remembered as a dedicated agent. After all, whatever happened in that last year, she gave seven centuries of loyalty to the Blades."

Jarrett had known his friend would see it that way. It was how he, Jarrett, had viewed the situation, as well. "It does matter."

Sam let out another long sigh. "I'll keep my ears open just in case, but I think you're right. It's time to put this behind us and move on. I appreciate you letting me know the truth though."

"Hey, we may not be partners anymore, man, but we'll always be brothers. You knew Cora even longer than I did. There's history there. I felt like you deserved to know."

Sam nodded, and then slammed his hand on the table. "So, on leave, huh? Headed off to parts unknown? Take that leaky tub of yours out to sea for a few weeks?" he asked, swiftly changing the subject and mood.

Six months ago, that is exactly what Jarrett would have done. But that was before his last leave, when he'd stayed in Nash to meet an informant with information on a possible sighting of Cora. He'd ended up helping his friend Fiona out on a case and meeting her sister, Anya. Now, two weeks alone on his boat didn't look as appealing as it always had before.

"I think I'll hang around town for a few days. It's been a while since I've spent time in Nash."

"Not so long, at least not compared to your usual comings and goings. I don't suppose your sudden interest in taking leave time has anything to do with a certain red-haired bartender?" Sam asked, a note of humor in his voice.

"And if it does?" Jarrett didn't bother pretending he didn't know what Sam was talking about. Neither did he wonder why Sam was asking. Though he and Anya had been discreet, Sam hadn't kept his job as the head of the Blades in Nash City for almost a hundred years by being unobservant.

"Need I remind you that Anya is like a niece to me?"

"Is this where I proclaim that my intentions are honorable?" Jarrett laughed.

"You could, but I'd know you were lying. Besides, I highly doubt Anya has ever had an honorable intention in her life, at least where a man is concerned, which is why I asked in the first place. I've never known you to dally with a norm, or to go back for seconds."

"Don't read more into it than there is, Sam. It's been a hard few months. I'm ready for a couple of weeks of relaxation. I just happen to be in Nash. Anya is my best friend's sister. I'm sure we will run into each other. If we do, we are both adults and can conduct our business accordingly." His tone was light, but there was an edge of warning to the last sentence.

Sam raised his hands in surrender. "Okay, I get it. It's none of my business. Just a warning though, Fiona might be your best friend, but she won't hesitate to kill you if you hurt her sister. I really don't want to have my best agent executed for murder. It would be a hassle replacing you, too."

Jarrett laughed. "Your concern for my welfare warms the cockles of my soul."

Sam grinned. "That's me, a big bundle of love and

concern."

Jarrett laughed again, truly enjoying his friend's company for the first time since he stepped into the office. "Yeah, you're a big bundle of something," he said, then ducked to avoid the file folder that whizzed past his head.

Four
Anya

"I don't date vampires," I said, my voice little more than a gasp as I pushed my hands under Jarret's shirt to get to the smooth skin beneath. I let my fingers play over the taught muscles of his back.

"This isn't a date," Jarret replied against my neck. His tongue traced a path from my chin to my ear.

That was true. Jarret was technically on duty for the Black Blade Guard. He was my bodyguard while my sister, his best friend, worked a case that potentially put my family in danger. So despite the fact that we had spent every waking moment together for the past few days, we weren't dating.

As I thought about what Jarret had said, I pulled

his shirt up over his head, giving my hands full access to his broad, muscular torso. I slowly ran my hands over his ridged stomach and up so that my palms grazed his tight nipples, eliciting a moan from the big man.

"I don't have sex with vampires, either," I said, holding my arms up so he could remove my shirt. A low moan forced its way through my lips as he lowered his mouth to my breasts, dropping soft, light kisses over each one. Then he moved to the nipples, sucking one into his mouth, laving it with his tongue, and nipping lightly with his teeth before moving to the other.

"And I don't have sex with my friends' sisters," he said in between nibbles. "I guess that makes us both a couple of rule breakers."

Jarret knelt in front of me, kissing my flat stomach as his hands slid up my thighs, under my skirt, and hooked onto my panties. He pulled them down in one agonizingly slow, sensual movement, and then lifted each of my feet to pull them off. "Are you sure no one will hear us?" he asked, his voice so thick and husky I could barely understand him.

I rolled my head back against the wall as he began kissing his way back up my torso. We were in the back storage room of Pinky's Pub. It was well past dawn and the pub was closed for business. "We should be fine. Fiona slept at Ian's last night and River has already gone to the market. Though Pinky is asleep upstairs, the noise-canceling spells will block any sounds, even from his vamp ears."

I stopped talking as his mouth returned to mine, and we melted together in a frenzy of tasting and exploring. I fumbled with the button fly of his pants until he pushed my hands away and quickly divested himself of the garment. With no effort at all, Jarret lifted me, his hands sliding under the smooth globes of my butt. I slid my legs around him, pulling myself tight against him as the hot, throbbing evidence of his desire nestled between my legs.

"Last chance to say no," Jarret said through clenched teeth.

"If you stop now, I will kick your ass," I retorted, sinking my teeth lightly into his earlobe.

Wordlessly, Jarret lifted me higher and positioned himself at my entrance. Then, with one hard, swift thrust, he was inside me.

I came awake on a gasp.

"Oh, shitballs!" My breathy exclamation reverberated in the quiet of the empty room. I clutched the sheet to my bare chest, breathing hard and trying to get my bearings. I was shaking, actually freaking shaking, from the dream. It had been so vivid and real, an almost exact memory of the first time Jarrett and I had been together a little over six months ago. Even now, I could almost feel the warmth of his touch, the scent of him, lingering on my skin.

I was losing my mind. That was it. There could be no other explanation. For some reason seeing Jarrett again had caused some sort of psychotic break. Yes, that was it. That too-hot-for-words kiss coupled with the fact that I hadn't had sex in six months had melted my brain and made me start having vivid, sweaty, leave-you-shaking sex dreams. This was just great.

Wait. Had it really been six months since I'd had sex? I sat in my bed, naked under my sheet, and thought about it. Yep, it really had been six months. I hadn't been with anyone since Jarrett. Not a single person. And it wasn't just sex. There hadn't been a make-out session, a sexy dance, or even a kiss. How was that even possible?

Well, it was no wonder I was having sex dreams about the hunky vampire. It was a surprise I wasn't having naughty dreams about every random man I met. Yet, I hadn't. Until now I hadn't even thought about it. Well, that wasn't completely true. I'd had more than a few fantasies about Jarrett in the first few weeks after our fling. But that was totally normal, nothing weird or obsessive. And the fact that I hadn't had sex, or even wanted to, with another guy since then meant nothing. I was growing up, maturing.

Yes, that was it. And it was only natural to be a little shook up after such a sexy kiss with no follow through. Okay, yes. It was all normal. It had nothing to do with Jarrett as a person. I had no particular attachment to him. None at all.

With that decided, I threw back the covers and crawled out of bed. Glancing at the clock beside my bed, I realized I'd been asleep less than six hours. It didn't matter. After that dream there was no way I was getting back to sleep any time soon. My skin still felt a little tingly and my whole body was buzzing. If I were seeing someone, I'd go find him and give him a wild ride to work out this excess energy. But since I'd just established that I hadn't had a guy on the line in six months, I'd have to find something else to do.

Dressing in a loose tank top and shorts, I went down to the training room on the third floor. The room was large, taking up half of the third floor, but sparsely decorated. A large, heavy bag hung on one end and a variety of weapons, weight training tools, and padded mats were lined up against one wall, but the rest of the room was empty, giving plenty of space for exercise and sparring.

I did some stretches to warm up, and then spent the next hour throwing kicks and punches at the heavy bag. When the last of the pent-up energy left my body, and I started to feel tired, I gave up the workout and went in search of humans and food.

I found River and Pinky downstairs in the pub's kitchen bottling honey-mead. Standing next to each other, my twenty-year-old sister and my over-two-centuries-old adoptive father looked like they were the same age.

"Hey guys."

River turned around, her smile wide. "Anya! You're up early."

I grabbed an apple from a bowl on the counter and bit in. "I've been up a little while, I couldn't sleep."

"Everything okay?" Pinky asked.

"Yeah, just weird dreams," I said, quickly adding, "Weird, not bad," when I saw Pinky's expression fill with concern. When I first came to live with him and my sisters, I had nightmares almost every night. For the first few months, he let me sleep in the backroom of the pub instead of upstairs so he could check on me throughout the night. I hadn't had a nightmare in years.

"Okay," he said. He pointed to my clothes. "You been working out?"

"Yeah. I figured I might as well do something constructive. You guys need any help?"

River placed three bottles of mead alongside several others on a rolling cart. "I don't think so. This is the last of the mead, and nothing else is ready to bottle."

"Do you need help setting up the bar? I didn't see Farrah around," I said, referring to the newest employee and resident of the pub. Farrah had been one of many victims in the case Fiona and Jarrett had worked on last year. For some reason, she hadn't been able to, or hadn't wanted to, return to her own home when she was released from the hospital after recovering from her wounds. Fiona, a consummate savior of kids in trouble, had asked Pinky to take Farrah in. At first, he had told her she could do a few chores around the pub for room and board, but she'd quickly started working full time cleaning the pub and helping River in her garden. She was also slowly becoming a part of the family.

"She already did most of the prep, but she's taking a nap right now. She'll be up in a couple of hours. Since it will probably be a pretty slow night and it's Gerald's night off, I figured it was a good time to start showing her the ropes of bartending. She should know how to do things so you can take off more than one night a week once in a while."

"Or so you can take a night off, ever."

"Bah, why would I want to do something crazy like that? I live to serve."

Pinky laughed as he said it, but it was truer than he probably would have admitted. Running the pub wasn't a job for him; it was a part of his nature. One only had to watch him in action to tell he truly enjoyed chatting with patrons, serving drinks, and laughing. Whenever Pinky was around, there was usually a lot of laughing.

I reached up and kissed his cheek. "You know what, you're right. Everything would probably fall apart around here if you took the night off."

He wrapped his arms around me in a tight hug. "Not with my Anya to keep things going."

I held onto him for a moment, savoring the feeling of safety and love that filled me when Pinky embraced me. After a few minutes I pulled away. "Okay, if you guys don't need me, I'm going to the bathhouse down the street to soak in some bubbles for about a gazillion hours."

"Oh, thank goodness," River said. "You really reek."

I stuck my tongue out at her, put my nose in the air, and turned and walked out with as much dignity as I could muster considering the fact that she was right. I stank.

I thought I was going to pass out from sheer boredom. When Pinky had predicted a slow night he'd grossly understated. At this pace, slow would be an incredible tempo increase. Other than the five regulars in the back playing poker and a young couple necking in a dark booth in the corner, the pub was empty. Pinky was at a table teaching Farrah the differences between the various alcoholic beverages we sold, pointing out the ones which were brewed in-house. The only thing that saved me from becoming comatose was my sister Fiona.

"So, when does Ian's night class let out?" I asked, hoping it wasn't until dawn. If she left, I'd have to resort to busywork like wiping down clean tables and sweeping the already clean floor, just to stay awake.

"In a couple of hours. I was expecting to be working tonight as well, but the raid we had planned was a bust. We went to the camp we'd been tipped on and found the slavers had skedaddled, if they even were slavers. It could have been a group of traders or gypsies. My money's on a band of merchants that stopped overnight before heading into the city for market week. It was a small campsite with evidence of only one wagon. Slavers would have had several. There would have been wheel tracks everywhere."

"Unreliable informant? Was it one of yours?" I asked, loving the conversation. I had gone through most of the same training at the Academy as Fiona, but my Norm status kept me from going into law enforcement in any capacity other than administrative. I wasn't the sit-behind-a-desk-all-day type, so I'd come to work for Pinky instead. Having Fiona tell me about the cases she was working on had always been a favorite part of my day. I'd really missed it since she'd hooked up with Ian. I'd never seen her so happy, though, so I couldn't begrudge her the time she spent with him. It just made me enjoy our conversations that much more.

"No. It came from someone the City Guard had arrested for assault. Apparently, he didn't want to pay for something he wanted at the market, and when the vendor took exception to his merchandise walking away, the guy attacked the vendor. He was trying to cut a deal for himself by saying he had information on a band of slavers."

I made a face. "I wouldn't be surprised if it had been some of his cohorts camping there."

"Very likely, and they cut and run when he was picked up. No matter. I'd much rather spend the evening chatting with you, and then snuggling with Ian, than wrestling sweaty slavers and doing paperwork." She sipped her wine.

I took a sip of my own ale. "Glad to hear I rate higher than sweaty slavers. That was a great visual, by the way."

Fiona grinned and opened her mouth to say something, but our attention was pulled to the door when it opened. A tall, dark-skinned vampire with a smooth, bald head and neatly trimmed beard entered. He walked across the room in a sexy, smooth stride.

"Luca," I said, grinning and genuinely glad to see my friend.

"Hi, Sweetness," he said, and pulled me into a tight hug.

His arms were warm and firm around me, and he smelled incredible, yet there were no stirrings in the pit of my stomach. This was a completely platonic hug.

"You changed that silly no vampire dating rule yet so you and I can get sweaty later?" he asked, dropping a light kiss on my cheek and letting me go.

"Not a chance," I quipped, moving out of the hug.

"Aww, come on, Baby Girl. Not even for me? Not even just once?" He put his hand over his heart in mock pain.

"Luca, you are the reason the rule exists in the first place," I teased, feeling a little twinge of guilt. I had broken the rule before, yet was not even tempted to do it again. At least, not with anyone new. Especially not with Luca.

My no-vampire-dating/sex rule had been born more out of practicality than any aversion to the race. Though everyone was welcome in Pinky's, the majority of our regular clientele were vampires. Not that I hadn't ever dated someone I met at the bar, but the rule made it easier to set boundaries. There was another reason, too. Vampires, especially those that had been around since before the Cataclysm, were odd creatures. Their unnaturally long lives caused them to go one of two ways, either chronically prone to one night stands, or lifetime monogamy.

Vampires could die, but there were no known diseases or natural causes that could result in the death of a vampire. And with their quick healing abilities, they were damned hard to kill. In the vampire world, a lifetime commitment basically lasted forever. Which meant a norm, like me, would have to be infected with the N-V virus and undergo "the big change." That was something I wasn't even remotely ready for. And since you never knew exactly what type of vampire you were going to get, it was better to stay away from them altogether.

I couldn't even try to think about why I had made an exception to the rule with Jarrett, but it could have been because I knew up front he was a classic roamer. He and my sister had been friends for more than half a decade and I hadn't even met him until six months ago. It seemed likely I'd never see him again. Of course, that way of thinking had come back to bite me in the ass this morning.

I should have foreseen that he'd roll through town on occasion, and it should be okay. I was friends with plenty of guys I'd once dated. Seeing Jarrett shouldn't push my libido into overdrive. The blame was on my lack of sex.

Surely once I got back in the dating game, having him pop up once in a while wouldn't keep playing havoc with my sleep. I wouldn't mind getting jazzed up over him if I weren't so positive that Jarrett Campbell was of the chronic, one-nighter variety. He probably hadn't spent more than one night with the same woman in three hundred years. It was too bad. Though I wasn't the kind to wait around for a guy, I wouldn't mind getting sweaty with Jarrett again on occasion, if I were unattached when he was in town

Luca Jensen, on the other hand, was another case entirely. The sexy, umber-skinned vamp had the smooth talk and charm of a bed-hopper, but there was something about him that made me believe at his heart, he was the one-woman-vamp type. A norm woman who got involved with him would have to be prepared to make the big change. That was definitely not me.

Instead of a potential romantic partner, Luca was one of my best friends. He knew my rule and respected it and me. For him, flirting with me was safe because he knew no matter what, we would stay platonic friends. As for me, I could enjoy his company and get all the relentless flirting and gratuitous ego stroking I wanted without any messy strings. It was really a win/win.

"Mead?" I asked, walking around the bar.

"Whiskey."

I shot him a glance. "Aren't you on shift?"

Luca was the head Med-Mage at City Hospital, the government medical clinic that catered to Blades, City Guard, and government personnel. He worked the night shift and usually came in for a mead on his hour break. He only drank whiskey on his nights off.

"I've been on shift since the start of my shift last night. We had a full class of trainees fresh from the Academy start their apprenticeships today. I spent the day in orientation with them, and then assigned them to the med-mages they'll be shadowing for the next year before they can go to other clinics in the city-state."

I knew vampires could go long periods of time without sleep, but I never really thought about how long. Pinky slept at least a few hours every day. The idea of being awake more than thirty-six hours exhausted me just thinking about it. "You should be home getting some rest."

He laughed. "Worried about me, Baby Girl? Don't be, I'm fine. I could have worked my full shift tonight, but the jittery energy of first-day interns tends to get to me after so many hours. I figured since I'm the boss, I could take off early and come knock back a few before heading home to bed."

I placed a shot glass in front of him and poured whiskey into it. "Leave the bottle," he said.

"Okay, but if you get so drunk you pass out in the middle of the floor, I'm not moving you. You'll wake up with boot prints on your pretty face."

He flashed a sexy grin. "Fair enough."

Of course he wasn't concerned. It would take much more than one bottle of whiskey to make him drunk enough to pass out. Vampire metabolism worked crazy fast on alcohol.

I kissed my palm and then blew it in Luca's direction. "You let me know if you need anything else," I told him with a wink, then went back to sit with Fiona.

"Sometimes I find it hard to believe the two of you never hooked up," Fiona said after I sat down.

I looked at her. "We're just friends. Besides, you know my vampire rule."

She gave me an odd look. "Yeah, I know."

There was no way in hell I was going to ask her what that look meant.

We sat together quietly for a few minutes before Fiona nodded to where Pinky and Farrah sat. Pinky had an assortment of bottles on the table in front of him and was pointing at each one while Farrah named them. "Those two seem to be doing well together," she said.

"Yeah, they get along pretty well. Pinky has hit a level of "Dadness" I haven't seen in a while. In addition to teaching her the ropes around here, he's helping her learn how to control her telekinesis. It's a lot like he was with us when we were kids, despite the fact that she is almost the same age as River."

Fiona smiled. "I was really counting on that. Farrah's biological father is a real scuz. Another fine example of wealth and power not equaling human decency."

I laughed. "I thought you'd gotten over your prejudice against the rich when you fell in love with the richest man in the city-state."

Fiona rolled her eyes. "I'm not prejudiced. Trust me, my feelings about Senator Purcell are purely based on his actions. Both he and Farrah's mother are norms, and they treated Farrah like her mage powers were a disease to be ashamed of. If you'd heard the way he'd talked about her when she was missing. He hadn't even wanted us to look for her. Ugh." She let out a snort of disgust.

I'd known there had to be something wrong with Farrah's home life when she came to live at the pub after her ordeal with the kidnapper Fiona had destroyed last year. I hadn't realized it had been that bad. My empathy and respect for Farrah went up a notch. I knew what it was like to have parents who detested who you were because you were different than them.

"That explains why she seems so surprised and even upset when her powers get stronger. She probably had to suppress them for years. I'll never understand the pure evil lurking inside some people. You were right to bring her here. Pinky will help her heal." *Like he did for me,* I thought, but didn't say it out loud.

"She was a bit of a brat before, from what I could tell. On the road to real destruction. But I think that was mostly due to her treatment at home. I had a feeling this would be a good place for her."

"Whatever she was like before, she's different now. She's quiet, never complains, and works damned hard. I've never seen this place shine like it does these days." I made a mental note to ask Farrah out for an afternoon of shopping and lunch soon. Unlike my sisters, she seemed like she'd enjoy doing girly things as much as I occasionally did.

"I'm glad you like her." Fiona grinned. "Now enough about her. I want to hear what's been going on in your life, little sister."

I shook my head. "Not much. Just working here and hanging out."

"Not fighting?"

I rolled my eyes at my sister's not-so-subtle poke. "Why tell you something you already know? I know you keep tabs with Pete. I'm doing as I promised. Only once a week and no juiced-up opponents."

"There are other fight-houses," she said.

"And you probably have at least one person in each reporting to you. And you know I'm not stupid enough to do the illegal fights. I'm not about to take on vampires or shifters. I fight for exercise and to relieve tension, not because I have an idiotic death wish." I took a deep breath, gearing up to really go on a tirade, when I saw the glint in Fiona's eye and the smile tugging at the corner of her mouth.

I clamped my mouth shut. She'd baited me and I hadn't fallen for it, I'd dove for it, head first. I grabbed my bottle of ale from the bar, took a swig, and then waved the bottle at her. "You are pure evil, you know that?"

Fiona stopped trying to hide her smile and broke into peals of laughter. "But you are so easy." She laughed so hard she snorted.

"Pure fucking evil," I murmured, taking another drink.

After a few minutes Fiona's laughter died down. "I'm sorry, I just miss you, and I really need someone to tease. Now that we are living together, it isn't as much fun giving Ian a hard time. He gets all sullen and pouty, and I have to be all sweet and beg for makeup sex to make him feel all manly."

I faked a gagging motion. "I will forgive you if you swear to never, ever, ever tell me that last part again. Ever."

Fiona grinned and took a sip of her wine. "Speaking of sex, have any encounters with any super-hotties lately?"

My thoughts flitted to my moment in the alley with Jarrett this morning. If anyone in the world qualified for super-hottie status, it was the giant vampire. Although I think they suspected it, I hadn't told either of my sisters about my fling with Jarrett. No need to go into it now. "Nope," I lied, feeling a twinge of guilt.

"Aww come on, Anya. Nothing? I'm doing this monogamy thing now; I gotta get my cheap thrills vicariously through you."

I laughed. "Geeze, Fee, when was the last time you had sex? You never acted this much like a sex-starved teenager when you were one."

"This morning." She laughed. "Okay, so maybe I lied, this monogamy thing is actually pretty damned awesome. You should try it sometime. You'd think it makes things boring, but trust me, it doesn't."

I shuddered. "Thanks, but you can have it. I have no desire to pin myself down with one man for more than a few weeks at a time. That is quite long enough for me to get bored."

"You really aren't seeing anyone?" Fiona asked, her voice edged with concern now. "It's been a while, hasn't it?"

Mercifully, at that moment the door swung open and a group of six women walked in. I waved at Pinky when he started to stand to let him know I'd take care of them. Then I drained the last of the ale from the bottle and hurried over to take the women's orders and escape my sister.

I was putting a round of drinks down on the table in front of the women and trying to figure out how to steer Fiona onto any other topic of conversation than my love life, when the door swung open again. I looked up and saw a tall, broad-shouldered vampire with long, dark hair and creamy brown eyes stride in. My hand shook as I set the last drink on the table. He was the last person I'd expected to see in the bar tonight.

FIVE
Jarrett

JARRETT STEPPED INTO PINKY'S PUB STILL NOT SURE it had been a good idea to come here. He'd floundered back and forth all afternoon about whether or not to stay in Nash, then all evening about whether or not to see Anya again. He hated being indecisive, and it had made him more than a little grumpy.

After leaving Sam's office, he'd gone to the market and restocked supplies, then grabbed a few hours of sleep. Once he got up, the indecision had started. He'd prepped the boat to leave before deciding he could leave tomorrow. He thought one night of fun in the city would do him good.

Until he saw Anya that morning, he hadn't

realized how long it had been since he'd had female companionship. Once he really thought about it, he realized Anya was the only woman he'd been with since he started tracking Cora.

Just one woman in a little over eight months. That wasn't completely unheard of. He had no hard and fast rules about having a little female companionship when he was working, mostly because he was always working. Often he was undercover in gangs of thieves and outlaws, and it helped sell his cover if he indulged in the available and willing women around him. He was a vampire after all, and had the over-active sexual appetite of any other of his race.

But as a Blade, he'd learned to control his urges better than most, and there were times when an assignment was so dangerous that being distracted by a woman for even a few minutes could get him killed. There were also those rare moments when he was so engrossed in a case that he didn't even think about sex or women. This had been one such time. But the case was over and his mind was free to think about other things. That had been why holding Anya close under that bridge today had kicked his libido into overdrive.

So, he'd dressed and went out to find some fun, but he hadn't headed for Pinky's. Instead, he went to a restaurant and bar near the docks, had a meal, and then moved into the bar area. Several women had approached him, though he couldn't chalk it all up to his good looks. Not that he was lacking in that area, but vampires produced higher amounts of pheromones than other humans.

But those women hadn't interested him, so he'd moved on to another bar. He'd gradually worked his way down Broadway, but every place had been the same. There had been many beautiful, willing women, but none that caught his interest. Once he'd realized that he kept looking for a particular shade of red hair paired with pale skin and a light smattering of freckles across the nose, he'd given up all pretenses and headed to Pinky's Pub.

The moment he laid eyes on Anya, his body kicked into high gear, telling him he'd finally made the right decision, though his brain was still not sure. Their eyes met and he saw the shock and interest flit across her features before she pasted on a generic, welcoming smile. He decided to stop listening to his brain for a while.

After her initial smile, she turned back to the women she was waiting on and Jarrett focused on finding a seat. He saw Fiona sitting at the end of the bar staring at him expectantly.

"When did you get back into town?" she asked after she'd hugged him and they were sitting down.

"This morning. Just finished wrapping up a case

and Nash was the closest place to report in," he told her, giving her his full attention.

"What can I get ya?" Anya asked, approaching them.

She was wearing a dark purple corset with a matching skirt of layered lace that ended mid-thigh. Black leather boots laced up to her knees. Her braided hair was wrapped around the top of her head, with tiny red tendrils escaping everywhere. She was mouth-watering.

Since Jarrett couldn't give the answer he wanted to with Fiona sitting right next to him, he said, "A whiskey would be great."

"No problem. Damn, I have to go get a bottle from the back. I'll be back." She turned and swished away.

"Jarrett."

"What?" He turned to Fiona. Apparently she'd been speaking.

"I asked you how long are you staying?" she said, smirking.

"I don't know. Not long, probably. I'm officially on leave. I haven't decided what I'll be doing just yet."

"I see. Well, I hope to see you before you leave," she said, pushing her wine glass away from her.

"You're leaving?" he asked, a little disappointed. It was true he hadn't expected to see her tonight, but he always enjoyed hanging out with Fiona. She was one of his few close friends.

"Yeah, Ian's teaching a night class that will be letting out very soon. I want to meet him at home. But don't pretend to look disappointed, I know I'm not who you came to see."

"I just came in for a drink," he lied. Badly.

Fiona laughed. "Oh, please. Don't even try that with me. I will admit that I was pre-occupied the last time you were in town, but I wasn't completely blind. Nor am I now. I know you have something going with Anya."

Busted. Jarrett scrambled for a moment, not sure how to respond, deciding on indirect honesty. "How do you feel about that?" he asked, not confirming or denying her suspicions, but not lying.

Fiona laughed and shrugged. "I didn't realize it was my business to feel any way at all. My sister is a big girl and can take care of herself. She has never come to me for approval of who she dates and would be pissed if I tried to give it. You, well, I think you can hold your own against her. Maybe." She gave him a wink.

Jarrett laughed. He shared her skepticism. "I was just asking out of respect. You are my best friend, and you do tend to go all over-protective-big-sister on occasion."

"Not this time." She laughed again before her expression sobered. "I love you like a brother, you know that right?"

Jarrett nodded. "Of course I do. And I love you, as well."

"And you know I'll always have your back, just like you've always had mine, right?"

He nodded. "Always."

"Good." Fiona stood up and moved behind him, wrapping her arms around him in a hug and pressing a light kiss on his cheek. She put her mouth next to his ear and in a low, soft voice said, "But just know, if Anya asked me to, and she had good reason and really meant it, I'd put a knife in your heart."

Her tone wasn't menacing but he knew she meant what she said. He had no doubt she'd attempt to do exactly as she described. And out of love for her, he'd let her succeed. "Fair enough."

"Good, just wanted to make sure we were clear," she said louder, her tone cheerful. Dropping another kiss on his cheek, she moved away. "Have a good night, I'll see you later."

She strode away as if she hadn't just threatened his life. God, he really loved that woman. It was like she was his twin, separated at birth. He watched as Fiona said her goodbyes to her family and then left the pub.

Was having another night with Anya worth pissing his best friend off and possibly losing his life? His eyes sought Anya and watched as she took a tray of drinks to the poker players in the back room. His eyes were drawn to the creamy, pale skin visible between the top of her boots and the hem of her skirt. Yep, he'd risk death. No doubt about it.

He was ruminating over his apparent death wish when Anya came back over, a bottle of whiskey and a shot glass in hand.

"I was going to bring this over a few minutes ago, but you were having a pretty intense conversation," she said, pouring a shot.

He downed the shot, savoring the warm burn at the back of his throat, and then put the glass back on the bar. "When is a conversation with Fiona not intense?"

She laughed and he felt it right down to his toes. Holy mother, everything about the woman was sexy as hell.

"True enough," Anya said. "Another?" She lifted the whiskey bottle.

He nodded. Yeah, he needed more. About a gallon more.

"So, I thought you were headed right back out of town after taking care of business this morning. Something else pop up?" she asked, a tiny glint in her eye.

Oh, yeah.

"I decided that since I'd saved you from three guys, I needed more of a reward," he said, slugging back the second shot.

Her eyes narrowed. "And just what kind of reward were you thinking to get?"

He wiggled the glass at her, flashing his sexiest grin. "The drink you promised me."

She poured another shot, but to Jarrett's surprise, she grabbed the glass and knocked back the amber liquid herself. Then she leaned across the bar, propping herself on her elbows and affording him a beautiful view of the creamy skin flowing out the top of her corset.

"I had a feeling you would be back."

"Oh? What made you think that?" he asked, leaning forward until their faces were only inches apart.

Her eyes danced. "The feeling I got against my hip when you had me pressed against the wall."

Jarrett burst into laughter. "I guess there isn't any use in trying to hide my true intentions then. So, what do you say? Want to take a walk with me when you get off work?"

She leaned closer, this time her breath tickled his ear as she whispered into it. "So, Vampire, you think you can just stroll in here after six months, flash me a sexy smile, and I'll let you back between my thighs?"

He pulled back, leaning against the back of the bar stool and grinning. "So, you think my smile is sexy?"

Her nose crinkled in mock-indifference. "It'll do."

He laughed again, took her hand, and ran his hand

over her palm. "So, are you telling me my smile isn't enough?" he asked. He loved this seductive game she was playing, though it really wasn't necessary. All she had to do was say the word and he would do whatever it took to have her in his bed, or on the bar, or in the back storeroom.

She looked down where their hands touched and back up at him, her eyes full of heat. "Oh, no, it is. I just thought I should pretend to be a little hard to get." She laughed and pulled her hand out of his. "But you'll have to wait. The bar doesn't close for another four hours, then I have to clean up."

"I've got nowhere to be," he said. Not for another two weeks now that he was officially on leave, but she didn't need to know that yet. Perhaps he wouldn't tell her at all. Maybe he would get his fill of her tonight, take off tomorrow night, and spend his two weeks leave somewhere else.

He watched as she walked to the other end of the bar, her skirt swishing across the tops of her thighs as her hips swung from side to side. He felt himself harden. Could he get his fill of her in one night?

Not bloody likely.

Six
Anya

I STOOD IN THE PUB'S KITCHEN, MY HANDS BRACED ON the counter top, trying to catch my breath. My heart was racing, and excitement and nervousness bubbled up inside me. It was odd. Flirting had never affected me quite this way. Flirting with the patrons was part of my job. And like Pinky, I was good at my job because it came second nature to me. Flirting was harmless and meaningless, but fun and made people feel good.

Of course I was good at the meaningful flirting as well. The seductive little games that lead to hot and sweaty horizontal games were also fun and exciting, but they never made my heart race like it did when I was playing them with Jarrett. When he had been here before, I had chalked the extra zing to the danger. After all, we had spent so much time together because he was protecting me from a deranged serial killer targeting people my sister loved.

But now, I was starting to think the danger came from the man himself. Jarrett Campbell intrigued me more than any other man ever had, and that in itself was dangerous.

"Do you know what you are doing?"

I gasped and jumped, grabbing a wine bottle like a club as I spun. I lowered it when I saw the intruder. "Shit, Pinky. You scared the crap out of me."

"Sorry," he said, but his tone and grin said he wasn't even a little sorry.

I put the wine bottle down. "What did you say?"

Pinky walked over and lazily leaned against one of the counters. "I asked if you know what you are doing."

"I'm putting dirty glasses in the sink," I said, confused.

Pinky rolled his eyes. "Not with the glasses, with Jarrett Campbell."

My head rolled back on my shoulders as I looked up at the ceiling.

"Damn vampire hearing," I muttered.

I took a deep breath and looked at my father. "No, I probably don't have a clue what I'm doing."

Pinky smiled. "Okay, I just wanted to make sure

you were aware of that fact."

I stared at him blankly. Pinky had never said anything to me about who I flirted, dated, or slept with. When my sisters and I were teens, Pinky had sat each of us down to talk about sex and responsibility. He'd always been open with us and given us the freedom to make our own choices. He never judged us when those choices turned out to be mistakes. He usually only stepped in if we were doing something that would hurt ourselves or each other.

"Am I going to get a lecture about hooking up with my sister's friend?" I asked.

He grinned. "Seems to me that if I were going to give you that lecture, I'm about six months too late."

My jaw dropped. "You know about that? How?"

Pinky gave me his best 'Dad' look. "You know, the sound proofing spells on this place might keep people upstairs from hearing what's happening down in the bar, but they have no effect on my keen sense of smell."

I felt my entire body flush crimson. "Crap on a cracker."

Pinky laughed. "Oh, don't be embarrassed. Really, you and your sisters keep a lot less from me than you think."

Which wasn't a hell of a lot, considering we pretty much told him everything.

"If it makes you feel any better," he continued,

"Fiona and Ian had sex in the rooftop garden one night while you, Jarrett, and I were playing cards down here."

I laughed. "Yeah, I actually knew that. River found her underwear tossed in the pumpkin patch." I took a deep breath and looked Pinky in the eye. "Okay, so you know Jarrett and I were together before. I'm sorry I tried to hide it."

Pinky came over and put his arm around my shoulder. "There's nothing for you to be sorry for. You are entitled to your privacy, and I strive to give you as much as possible. I only brought it up because I wanted to make sure you were aware that you were venturing into territory you've never been in before."

"You mean because Jarrett is a vampire? Or because he is Fiona's best friend?" I asked, leaning my head on his shoulder.

"Both. Plus the fact that I've never known you to hook up with someone again after an affair has ended."

"You think I have some sort of emotional attachment to Jarrett?" I asked.

Pinky stepped back so he could meet my eyes. "I don't know one way or the other. What do you think?"

"I think Jarrett is a nice guy. We had a lot of good talks when he was here. I also think he is sexy and exciting, and the sex was phenomenal. I wouldn't mind doing that again. And the passage of time between encounters has to do with nothing more than the fact that he just happened to come back to town and I have nothing else to do. That's all there is to it."

"Okay."

"Okay? That's all? You just wanted to make sure I wasn't being all stupid and getting my heart involved?" I shook my head, not understanding this conversation at all.

"There is nothing stupid about getting your heart involved in a relationship. The fact that you think there is concerns me a little. I just wanted to make sure you were aware your heart could get involved, and it might not have the results you would expect."

"So you think that because we are friendly, and because I've been with him before, if I hook up with Jarrett I might be sad when he leaves again. Or that I might feel weird when I see him again, as I'm likely to do because he and Fiona are friends."

Pinky nodded. "It could happen. How do you think you'll deal with it if it does?"

I shrugged. "I'm not the type to feel weird about guys I've slept with, and I have never felt sad about a guy. But, I suppose it *could* happen. If it does, I'll get over it."

Pinky laughed and bent to drop a light kiss on my forehead. "That's my pragmatic girl."

He stepped over, took a tray of glasses I'd just washed, and put them on a shelf before turning back to me. "That group of women just left in a huff after each of them propositioned Jarrett and were turned down. They started towards Luca, but I guess he didn't like being second best, because he took his drink and went back to play poker."

I laughed. "Poor drunk bitches. I had a feeling they'd do something like that."

"It's beyond dead in there. I think Farrah and I can handle the rest of the night if you want to head out a little early."

"You came back here to question me about my sex life, then let me off work early so I can go have sex?"

"Yep."

I shook my head in exasperation. "You are the weirdest father on the planet."

He flashed a grin. "I'll take that as a compliment."

I ignored him and went out the door and up the back steps to the fourth floor apartment I shared with River. In my bedroom, I quickly stuffed a change of clothes and pair of sandals into my bag. It might be presuming too much, but there was little doubt in my mind that 'take a walk' was code for 'have hot monkey sex', and I wanted to be prepared. I grabbed a shawl and headed back downstairs, this time using the front stairs that emptied directly into the bar area.

Sitting on the stool next to Jarrett, I grabbed his glass and poured myself a shot from the bottle I'd left him. "So, you ready to go for that walk?" I asked, pretending the warmth in the pit of my stomach was only a side-effect of the liquor.

※

Like the pub, the street outside was nearly deserted. On a busy night, the sidewalks would be packed with people shopping or going to the bars and taverns that lined Broadway. Pinky always said that, with the exception of a few buildings that had been destroyed, this street was much like it had been before the Cataclysm. Tonight, there were only a couple dozen people milling up and down both sides of the wide street. A few for-hire rickshaws were parked next to the sidewalks, waiting to take patrons wherever they needed to go.

Jarrett looked down at my feet, and then motioned towards one of the rickshaws near the pub's entrance. "Those don't look like they were made for walking. Do you want to take a ride instead?"

I pulled the knitted shawl around my bare shoulders to block out the cool night air. "I take it you have a particular destination in mind. Is it far?"

It was my guess that the destination would be his room at Blade's Headquarters, which was barely two blocks away. Or perhaps he'd rented a room at one of the inns on Broadway, which also wouldn't be far.

"A few blocks," he said.

"Then I'll be fine. It's a nice night for a walk," I said. Both Fiona and River often lamented my habit of wearing high heels to work, especially since Fiona had borrowed some of my clothes a few months ago when she'd been undercover. She'd had a hard time getting used to walking in my shoes. But I enjoyed heels, they made me feel feminine. The knee-high, spike-heeled boots I was wearing were a pair of my favorites. "But, I can go change if you think there will be a problem."

One side of his mouth quirked up in a wicked, sexy grin. "Don't you dare."

A tiny thrill flitted through me. "Then lead on."

Jarrett laced his fingers with mine and we started walking. We didn't talk. Instead, we enjoyed a companionable silence, as if we really were just out for an evening stroll. Yet, I knew there was a purpose to this walk and giddy anticipation buzzed through me.

I was surprised when we left the bars and inns behind us and crossed the street to the docks. The Cumberland River was a main trade and travel access point in and out of Nash. It was busy at all hours, day or night. While the area wasn't as bustling as it had been that morning, there were still numerous dock workers, sailors, and fishermen loading and unloading barges and fishing boats. Solar-crystal lanterns illuminated the docks and ships with a soft, blue glow.

Wondering what he could possibly want to show me on the river in the dark, I quietly followed him down the dock until we stood in front of a sailing ship that looked to be around fifty feet long. It was well taken care of, but I could tell it was quite old. Mostly because the design and materials were nothing like any other boat I'd ever seen on the river. It was missing the steam-powered paddle-wheel all the wide, flat barges used to propel themselves up and down the river. Instead, it had a large pole with an attached sail shooting out of the front, high into the air, resembling the smaller versions on the fishing boats. This boat was also about twice their length, and the deck was nearly even with the top. In the center was a room surrounded with windows, and there was an area raised about three feet over the deck. On the side, "The Minnow" was painted in bright red letters.

"Is this the boat you came in on today?" I asked.

"It is. Actually it's my boat. My home."

I felt my eyes go wide. "Your home? You live on a boat? That's kind of cool."

He laughed. "I don't disagree. Want a tour?"

"Absolutely!"

He laughed and helped me aboard. We went into the windowed room first.

"This is the wheelhouse," Jarrett said. "It's where I

steer and run the boat."

I looked around. Seats lined the sides and the front wall. To one side was a dashboard with levers, dials, and a spoked wheel. There were two doors low in the wall on either side of the room.

Jarrett went through a door and downward. He peered up at me through the opening. "Be careful on the stairs."

I followed him into a room with built-in cupboards on one side and a table and benches built into the other side.

"As you can see, this is the dining area. And this is the galley, or kitchen as you would call it," he said, stepping through another doorway. "And through that door is a small cabin I use for storage."

I followed him into the narrow room that had cabinets built on both sides. It had a sink, a small crystal-stove, and several cabinets overhead. "This is wonderful." I said, running my hand over the gleaming, polished wood.

"It's home," he said, but his eyes brightened. I could see he was pleased I liked his space. He brushed past me and walked back to where we started. I followed him up the stairs back into the wheelhouse. He pointed at the other door. "Through there is the head and two more cabins, including mine, which I'll show you later," he said, his voice dropping into a sultry timbre on the last few words.

"The head?" My curiosity was more powerful than his seductive ways.

He laughed. "The bathroom."

My eyes widened. "You have a bathroom on your boat?"

His eyes twinkled. "It's kind of a necessity, even for vampires. It has a working shower too. I'll show you how to use it later," he said, but this time he was laughing too hard to be seductive.

His laughing was due to my eyes growing even wider when he'd said "working shower." I'd never taken an actual shower before. Pinky had told us about them, but plumbing just wasn't what it once was. We didn't even have running hot water in the pub. We used a bathhouse a few blocks away, soaking in tubs of hot water to bathe. I tried to imagine water cascading down my body.

I didn't realize I'd closed my eyes until I heard Jarrett clear his throat.

"Sorry, I was imagining a shower. I've never had one."

His eyes were dark and seductive. "That must have been one heck of an imagining, you were moaning like you were being caressed."

My face burned with embarrassment. "I guess I was, by water."

He laughed again. "Okay, before I get sidetracked, want to go for a ride?"

"Oh, can we?" I asked, not caring that I sounded like a five-year-old asking for candy. "It's so dark and there isn't any wind."

Jarrett touched his hand to a crystal on the dashboard and several crystal lanterns popped to life around the edge of the boat, casting the water with a blue-tinged glow. Then he took a small crystal from his pocket and pushed it into a depression next to the gears on the dash. A soft rumbling started below our feet.

"Water-crystal engine. It works great for navigating the river," he said.

I watched as he went out and untied the boat from the dock and moved around the deck, preparing to sail.

"I love your boat," I said when he came back into the wheelhouse and sat in the tall chair behind the steering wheel. "It's really beautiful."

"She," he said.

"What?"

He smiled. "A boat is a she, not an it. It's an old sailor thing, humor me."

"Okay, then. She is beautiful," I said, running my hand across the polished wood. "How old is she?"

He turned the wheel and we began moving out into the middle of the river. I stumbled back and fell into the seat next to the window.

"Are you okay?" he asked.

"I'm fine, just never been on a boat like this before. Actually, I don't think I've ever been on a boat at all." If I had, it was when I was too young to remember, though I doubt I had, even then. The gypsy tribe I grew up in before Pinky had found me had stuck to the woods and mountains of Appalachia. We'd gone to the banks of the Mississippi Sea, as well as the Atlantic Ocean in Atlanta, but we'd never attempted to sail on them.

Concern flashed across Jarrett's face, and then was gone. "Okay, but let me know if you feel queasy or anything. I might have some herbs in the galley that will help."

"I'm fine. Now answer my question." I smiled at him in the dim blue glow of the lantern.

He turned his attention back to the water, watching where he guided the boat as we slowly moved through the water. "Well, she was originally built around three hundred years ago, give or take a decade. I found her about sixty years later in a junk yard. She had a hole in her hull and was in pretty rough shape. Whoever owned her had erased her name, taken her maintenance records, stripped off everything of value, and left her to rot."

He patted the wheel as if petting a beloved dog. I didn't quite understand it, but I found it endearing. I experienced a pang of regret on The Minnow's behalf.

"That's horrible," I said, meaning it. "So you restored her?"

"Yes. I restored her as close to original as I could come without having her records. And, since I couldn't find any record of her original name, I renamed her. But over the years, I've made some major modifications to her," he said, and I could hear a tinge of regret in his words.

"What kind of modifications?"

He sighed. "The Minnow was built as a cruising yacht. Her only source of power was a diesel engine. When the Paranorm Council informed the Blades of the Cataclysm predictions and warned us to start taking precautions, I knew diesel would eventually become scarce, and then non-existent. I modified her to be a sailing ship. She already had a mast and boom, so it wasn't as hard as it could have been. Later, I had a mage help me modify the motor to a water-crystal-powered engine like the ones used in rickshaws and surreys today, but more powerful. Also, I can use sea or river water, so I never run out of fuel."

"That's really cool," I said, not sure what else to say. It was clear he really loved his boat. And I didn't blame him. It, she, was beautiful and had obviously been his home for centuries. *How nice it must be to have a home that could take you almost anywhere*, I thought. Then, I was shocked at myself. I had a home like that once, a wagon, and it had never brought me any happiness. Though I had to admit, my miserable childhood had nothing to do with where I'd slept. I had enjoyed traveling from place to place. It was the people I'd had to travel with that I could have done without.

No, I told myself silently. I would not let thoughts of my childhood ruin this lovely night on the river with Jarrett. I pushed them out of my head and looked out at the dark water and the lights of the city beyond.

As we neared the edge of the city, Jarrett touched the scry-crystal on the dash next to the wheel and gave his name, rank, and a series of numbers. "The Minnow requesting departure."

A male face appeared on the small screen and said, "You have clearance to depart through the East river gate."

Jarrett powered down the crystal, then seeing my look of confusion, explained. "Even though the river gates rarely get closed anymore, the guard towers still monitor traffic in and out of the city. Smaller fishing and trade vessels that don't carry scry-crystals have to stop at the check-in station." He pointed to a long, floating pier with a small wooden guard shack built on the end. "There's another on the other side for incoming traffic."

"Wow, I've lived in this city over a decade now and

that is the first time I've ever been in this area. I had no idea that was how the gates worked," I said, awe in my voice.

"Only a decade? Where did you live before?" he asked, curiosity creasing his forehead.

"More than a decade, probably closer to fifteen years now. And as for before, I think that's a story for another time," I said, feeling a twinge of guilt for not sharing with him after he'd told me about The Minnow. But I didn't want my past to cast a shadow on our lovely evening.

"No problem," he said nonchalantly. "Look over there, there are some kids night fishing on the rocks by the gate. It's technically illegal because it's dangerous, but the patrols usually ignore them. The fish gather around the rocks and wall, making for really good fishing."

I looked where he was pointing and could just see three small figures on the rocks below the glowing crystal lights that marked the wall. "That is actually something I knew. Fiona used to go fishing by the western gate. I stayed home with River. I had no desire to touch stinky, slimy fish."

His laugh was rich and velvety. "Note to self, don't take Anya fishing."

My own laughter joined his.

We sailed on for several minutes before he pulled

closer to the shoreline, slowed, and then turned off the crystal-engine.

"What are you doing?" I asked.

"Weighing anchor," he said, moving to the other end of the boat and doing things I couldn't see in the dark, though I heard a splash.

"Oh. Why?"

"My intention had been to bring you out so you could see the sunrise; it's beautiful as it shines across the river. But I didn't anticipate you getting off work early. We still have a few hours until then."

"Is it safe to stay here?"

"Yes. We are well out of the way of any other boats that might be navigating the river."

I looked towards the dark shoreline only a few yards away, then back towards the city where the glow of the night lights was barely visible beyond the trees and the wall. He must have seen the doubt on my face because he added, "I also have some pretty strong shield and alarm spells. They'll alert us if anyone gets within two feet of the boat, as well as give the intruders a pretty nasty shock."

I knew the types of spells he was talking about. We had the same thing at the pub. The shield on the front door was only active during closing hours, but the back door and all the windows, as well as a perimeter around the rooftop where my sister grew her gardens, had permanent shield spells powered by crystals that were charged regularly. They were tuned to the energy of those of us living in the building. We could pass through safely at any time, but if someone else tried to come through, they'd get shocked and thrown back several yards. A second attempt would knock them unconscious.

Everything I knew about Jarrett told me that his shields were even more powerful than ours. I had no doubt we would be completely safe here, even without the nominal protection being inside the city walls gave.

"So, we still have at least two hours before dawn," I said.

He grinned and leaned back against the wall. "Yep, two very long hours."

I stood and walked over to him, sliding my hand seductively up his chest. "I guess we'll have to find a way to pass the time," I purred in my most coquettish voice.

He didn't need any further invitation.

SEVEN
Anya

JARRETT GRABBED ME AND PULLED ME AGAINST HIM, his mouth coming down on mine. All pretense was gone. The kiss started out hot and heated up with every passing second. I slid my arms around his neck, tangling my fingers in his hair. Sliding his hands under my bottom, he lifted me up.

"Wrap your legs around my waist and hold on," he growled into my neck.

"My pleasure," I replied, doing as he'd ordered.

He moved towards the door we hadn't gone through earlier and deftly navigated the steep stairs with me pressed against his chest. Within seconds I was deposited on a wide bed that seemed to be built into the wall. I let go as he leaned back, left me on the bed, and peeled off his shirt. My mouth went dry.

"I don't want to be crass, but I need to get out of these clothes. I'm not sure how much playing I can do the first time, I want you pretty badly."

Hot balls of fire ricocheted through me. Whether it was that he said "first time" or the pure need in his voice, I was definitely in sync with his feelings. As he stripped, I made short work of my own clothes, thanking my lucky stars the corset I'd chosen to wear tonight had hook and eye closures in the front so I didn't have to endure the time-consuming chore of unlacing it.

After tossing my clothes aside, I paused to watch Jarrett as he pulled off his boots and pants and then walked towards me. Damn the man was glorious. Tall, broad shouldered, and every inch of him packed tight with muscle. Every single inch. I shivered, knowing I was as ready for him as he was for me.

I reached down to start the process of removing my boots when he said, his voice thick, "Leave them on."

I grinned up at him and leaned back, feeling sexier than I ever had in my life. I spread my legs in invitation and before I could blink, he was there, kneeling between my thighs, holding himself above me with one arm on either side of me. I slid my arms around his back, loving the feel of his smooth skin and hard muscles. I pulled him down so that his chest pressed against my breasts.

"I don't need a lot of play either, I just need you," I told him.

He leaned back and looked down at me, his gaze smoldering. "Well, a little play," he said, a sexy smirk curving his lips, and then his mouth was on mine, drinking me in, before sliding down to my ear and throat.

"Don't..." I started.

"Don't bite. I know." He pulled his mouth away from my neck and looked up at me, his eyes burning with desire. "Don't worry, I don't think either of us needs to be drugged to make this feel good."

He punctuated his last statement by moving his mouth to my breast and grazing it with his teeth. Alternating from breast to breast, he sucked and licked until I thought I'd turn into ashes. "Enough, Jarrett. Now, please."

He gave a sensual, husky laugh. "Demanding little thing, aren't you?"

"Yes," I gasped, digging my fingers into his back and pushing my hips up to him.

He groaned with pleasure and wordlessly slid into me. We moved together, our hands and mouths touching, tasting, and exploring as we plummeted towards release. It could have been hours, it could have been mere minutes. I wasn't sure. Time had evaporated. All I knew was the feel of Jarrett against me and in me. Then heat engulfed me, my body tensed, and wave after wave of intense pleasure washed over me. Without realizing what I was doing, my nails dug deeper into his back and my teeth sank into his shoulder. A few moments later, Jarrett's muscles clenched under my fingers. He groaned, thrusting harder into me with his own release.

We lay side-by-side in the bed for a long time, neither of us talking, just trying to catch our breaths. After a while, Jarrett broke the silence with a chuckle.

"So, no biting, huh?"

I grimaced. "Sorry about that."

He laughed softly and ran a finger up my arm, sending tingles of excitement through me. "There's nothing for you to be sorry for. I liked it." He shot me a sexy grin.

I shrugged, laughing. "Well, there is that. It's still a little hypocritical of me."

Leaning on one elbow, he looked down at me, his face serious. "No, Anya, it's not. You biting me and me biting you are two very different things. I don't drink human blood, norm or vampire, under most circumstances. But I can't deny that doing so during sex heightens the pleasure for both parties."

I nodded. "Because vampire saliva is a drug to humans and human blood is a drug to vampires. And vampire blood is more intoxicating than norm blood. I know that. The bars are full of suckers just aching to get bit."

He smiled at me. "Exactly. But I am one of the rare vampires who finds exchanging blood to be an extremely intimate act. I might nip at your skin with my teeth, but I will never extend my fangs and bite you. Not unless you ask me to. And then, only if I want to do so." His grin turned lecherous. "But you can feel free to sink your tiny little teeth into me anytime you want. I like it."

"Humph!" I swung my leg out to kick him and the heel of my boot got tangled in the sheets. "Oh, crap, I forgot I had these on. I should take them off before I rip your sheets or poke a hole in your mattress."

I started to sit up, but he gave me a gentle push back onto the mattress.

"Let me," he said.

He moved so that he was kneeling at my feet and reached for the boot on my right leg. He slowly unlaced the boot then slid it off, his hands sliding over every inch of my leg on the way down. He moved to the second boot, giving it the same treatment.

Then, starting at my ankle, he began kissing and licking his way up my leg. It was so hot and sensual, my entire body buzzed. When his lips and tongue were mere inches from the apex of my thighs, I braced myself for the sensations I was sure would come next. Instead, he retraced his way back down my leg. I moaned my frustration as he started up the other leg in the same manner. This time as his mouth moved across my inner thigh I wasn't disappointed. I shook with pleasure as his tongue flitted over my most sensitive spot, and then I groaned as he slid one finger inside me.

I wrapped one hand in the long, silky strands of his hair, while the other clutched at the sheets beneath me. I writhed under him, letting the sensations rock me as he licked and stroked me into delirium. Unable to stop myself, I screamed out his name as my orgasm shook me.

Within seconds, he was over me, pushing his hard length into my body. I welcomed him, arching up to meet him. He immediately began to move, hard and fast. My nails dug into his back as I met him thrust for thrust. To my surprise, it only took a few minutes before I was there again, in that storm of pleasure that took my breath away as my body tightened and clenched around him and the world broke into a million tiny pieces.

Several hard strokes later he growled his own release into my neck.

EIGHT
Jarrett

"We missed the sunrise," Anya said, stretching like a satisfied cat.

"Yes, I guess we did." Jarrett leaned up on both elbows to watch her as she walked around the cabin picking up her discarded clothing, apparently unbothered by her nudity.

Jarrett, on the other hand, was very bothered. He could feel himself hardening again as he took in her creamy skin and tantalizing curves. He had to force himself to stay in control. They'd already made love several times over the past few hours, and though he was ready and willing for more, he wasn't sure Anya would be. It had been so long since he'd been with a non-vampire, and Anya's sexual appetite was so voracious. He'd almost missed the signs of how tired she was until she started yawning a few minutes ago, shortly after their latest tumble around the bunk.

"So, are you headed off to parts unknown this afternoon?"

She had her back to him as she found the last bits of her clothing and began to dress. He couldn't see her expression. Nor could he gauge her mood from her voice. He was silent a long moment, watching her pull on her skirt and trying to decide how to respond. When she sat on the bench to pull her boots onto those sinfully long and sexy legs, he quickly made up his mind about how he wanted to spend the next two weeks.

"Actually," he said, keeping his tone as neutral as possible. "I'm on leave for the next two weeks and will probably be hanging around Nash City. So, I'll be around if you want to try to catch that sunrise, or whatever."

She looked at him hard for one long moment, dropping her boot on the floor. She strode over to the end of the bunk.

"Jarrett Campbell," she said, slowly crawling up the bed, her legs on either side of his. "Are you asking me if I want to spend the next two weeks screwing your brains out every chance I get?"

"I..." but he couldn't finish the sentence. She had

pulled the sheet away from his erection and was lightly running her fingers up and down. It was everything he could do to keep his eyes from rolling back in his head.

"Because if you are…" She moved up, straddling his hips, and he suddenly realized she hadn't put her underwear on yet.

"The answer is…" She positioned him at her opening.

"Yes." The word was drawn out on a breathless gasp as she pushed down.

Forty-five minutes later, Jarrett pulled The Minnow alongside the pier he'd been moored at earlier. He'd barely finished securing the lines when Anya gave him a quick kiss and climbed ashore.

"It will be busy tonight so it will be almost dawn before I can leave work. I'll see you," she said with a wink. Then, tossing her long red locks over her shoulder, she turned and disappeared into the crowd of sailors, fisherman, and other dock workers.

He watched her go, wondering just what he'd gotten himself into. The woman was likely to drive him mad before two weeks was up. At least he didn't have to worry about staying busy. He looked around at The Minnow. He'd neglected her over the past several months while he'd been obsessed with his quest for Cora. There was plenty of scrubbing, scraping, painting, and repairing to do around the boat. He pushed Anya and her amazing body out of his mind and went to get supplies and get started.

※

Three days later, Jarrett knew Anya wasn't lying beside him the moment he reached consciousness. It vaguely registered in his brain how, in the past three days, he was already used to waking up with her warm body against his. He opened his eyes to the dim light of early dusk peering through the cabin's narrow windows. Next to him, the bed was bare as he'd suspected, but it only took a second to find Anya. She was standing at the end of the bunk, fully dressed with hat and bag in hand, tiptoeing towards the door.

"Where are you going?"

Anya gasped and turned around, a guilty look on her face. "I wasn't sneaking out."

She was so adorable while trying to be sneaky. He leaned up on one elbow. "Of course you weren't. So, where are you going? I know you aren't going to work, you're off tonight."

She let out a sigh. "Pete's Fight House."

He climbed out of bed and began to dress. "You thought I'd disapprove?"

Her eyes narrowed. "It doesn't really matter what you think."

He laughed, loving the tinge of pink that filled her cheeks and the fire that flashed in her eyes. "True, it doesn't. Can I go with you?"

The pink deepened and her eyes narrowed. "I don't need you to protect me."

"Wow. You know, it's times like this that I really see the family resemblance between you and Fiona. That fierce independence would be attractive if you weren't so quick to jump to conclusions and be defensive. I merely thought it would be fun to watch you fight. Fiona has told me you are a better fighter than she is, but I haven't had the chance to see it myself." He thought it best not to point out that just a couple of days ago she had, indeed, needed protection.

She had the grace to look slightly chastised before her attitude snapped back into place and she rolled her eyes. "Don't get your panties in a bunch. You can come with."

With a single stride, he crossed the room, grabbed her by the waist, and picked her up. Her legs automatically went around him, her boots knocking against the back of his thighs. Her arms wrapped around his neck as his hands slid under her bottom. Pushing her against the nearest wall, he kissed her hard and hungrily.

When they were both breathless, he pulled his mouth away, kissing across her cheek to her ear where he traced the lobe with his tongue. "Good morning," he whispered, nipping her ear with his teeth.

She let out a little moan. "Oh, yes. Good morning. You know, going to Pete's could wait until tomorrow."

He slid his hands back up to her waist and pulled her away from him. He set her back on her feet and took a step back. "No, we'll go. I'm in the mood to see you kick some ass."

She swayed a bit and leaned back against the wall and glared at him. "And suddenly I'm in the mood to do just that," she said through gritted teeth.

She looked so volatile and sexy, it was everything he could do not to scoop her back into his arms and take her back to bed. Maybe he shouldn't have teased her. She'd deserved it trying to sneak out on him, but it had tortured him as much as her.

He picked up her hat and bag from where she'd dropped them. "Come on, Killer, let's go see what kind of trouble you can get us into."

She stared daggers at him for another moment before her mouth curved into a slow, sexy smile. "You are going to pay for that later."

"I'm looking forward to it."

Pete's Fight House was illuminated by a mixture of crystal and oil lanterns casting a dim, blue glow over a massive crowd that had gathered to watch the evening's fights. Jarrett stood ringside, watching as Anya moved gracefully around the ring, throwing punches and kicks and dodging blows. He'd known, from nights of exploring her luscious body, how muscular and athletic she was, but watching her toss her opponent around and bounce up when she was knocked down told him she had a strength he hadn't imagined.

She was magnificent, moving with a practiced grace he'd seen in few fighters. The fact that she wasn't paranorm made it all the more phenomenal. Vampires and shifters were stronger with faster reflexes, and some mages could use magical energy to increase their agility. But Anya had none of that. Her abilities came from training and practice.

He wondered what made her work so hard on her body. And, even more, why did she fight? He fought as a part of his job, though he couldn't deny he enjoyed it. But that was partially due to the vampire side of him. Vampires were adrenaline junkies, and fighting was one of the best activities to get his kicks. But Anya had no such compulsion. He wondered what pain or trauma from her past drove her to fight for sport.

Barely four minutes after the match began, Anya had her opponent's shoulders pinned to the floor as the referee counted down. The crowd of spectators roared with approval as Anya was announced the winner. Jarrett couldn't help smirking at the name "Spitfire" as the ref called it out. He knew Anya must hate it, but it fit her so perfectly. She did everything with a fiery passion that matched her hair color.

His own temperature started to rise with thoughts of having her and all that blazing passion in his bed later. But, his ardor cooled drastically a few seconds later when a man entered the ring and challenged her before she could exit.

"Come on, Spitfire," the man said. "Your other opponents tonight barely had enough skill to warm you up. I'll be a little tougher to put down."

Jarrett groaned. The man was well over six feet tall, probably no more than an inch shorter than Jarrett. He was also at least fifty pounds heavier and nearly solid muscle. Unlike many of the big men Anya and Jarrett had watched fight tonight, he carried himself with the grace of a trained fighter. He wouldn't be as easy to put down as the previous two were. Surely Anya wouldn't be daft enough to go into a third match against someone who hadn't fought at all tonight and clearly had the physical advantage.

"Let's do it," Anya said.

Jarrett groaned. Of course she was that daft.

"Are you sure you want to do this?" Jarrett asked when she'd joined him to rest a minute and wait for bets on the fight to be placed.

"Sure. Why not?" she said, wiping sweat from her face with a towel.

"Um, I don't know, maybe because you've already fought twice and the dude's as big as a building." Jarrett gave her his best 'that was an idiotic question' eye roll.

She returned his eye roll with her own. "I've got this."

She tossed the towel down and went back to the ring so that the ref could announce the fight.

The bell rang and as soon as the fight started, Jarrett knew he'd been right about the man's training. He and Anya were evenly matched in skill, plus he had the advantage of having observed her fighting style in her first two fights. They traded blows for a few minutes, but it wasn't long before the big man had the upper hand.

It took everything Jarrett had in him to stand still and watch as the man's huge fists came into contact with Anya over and over. He landed three solid punches, one to her jaw, two to her stomach. Then his heavy booted foot swept out and knocked her legs from underneath her. With a grunt and cry of pain, Anya fell to the ground, blood and sweat flying. Jarret lifted his foot to rush to her, but Pete's arm slammed across his chest, stopping him in his tracks.

"She won't thank you for it, Son."

At any other time Jarrett would have laughed at

the gravelly voiced old man calling him son. Despite his visible age, he was more than five hundred years younger than Jarrett. But as it was, Jarrett's mind was filled with the need to protect Anya. As he put his hand on Pete's arm to move it, the old man spoke again.

"Seriously, boy. Just hold on a minute. Anya knows what she's doing. She can take care of herself."

Brushing the man's arm aside, Jarrett took a step forward anyway, stopping dead in his tracks when Anya lifted her head and met his eyes. He saw a ferocity he'd never seen before, and he knew that Pete had been right. If he stepped in and stopped the fight, Anya would be furious with him. He took a step back to his original place next to Pete, ignoring the man's soft snort of laughter.

Anya slowly and deliberately pulled herself to her knees. It was apparent she was in some pain, but from the vitality he'd seen in her eyes, Jarrett was sure she was putting on a show to make her opponent think she was feebler than she was. Before she could reach her feet the man's foot swept towards her mid-section. Jarrett barely had time to think what a low blow it was before Anya turned, grabbing the man's boot seconds before it made contact with her ribs. She grasped it in both hands as she used her legs to propel herself to her own feet, pulling the man's leg up with her. Once she was up she gave the boot a hard twist and the giant went crashing to the ground.

Instead of kicking the man while he was down, Anya stood back and waited for him to gain his feet. She stood at the center of the ring, arms loose, slightly tilted to the side as if she were favoring her left leg, head down. She looked like she was hurt and trying to catch her breath, and she probably was. But Jarrett was certain she wasn't quite as hurt as she appeared. Despite the apparent looseness in her stance, and her unclenched hands, a tense alertness vibrated off her.

Her opponent gained his feet and went straight for her, swinging. She stood still until the last moment, then crouched, bending at the knee, and ducked his fist. Her own clenched fist shot up, pummeling his stomach three times fast. Then she rose, catching his chin with another blow. The next minute or so consisted of Anya ducking almost all of her opponent's swings and kicks, and landing almost all of her own. She danced about in a fury unleashing all of her rage and frustration on the man.

Though she was using the skill and precision she'd had in her earlier fight, there was something hard and dark in the way she fought now. Something that could only come from a place of deep pain. Jarrett found himself wondering again what could have happened to Anya to make her fight with such edgy ferocity, and how he could soothe the pain away.

But that thought was quickly lost as Anya delivered a roundhouse kick to her beast-sized opponent's head and he fell onto his back. He was still one long moment then raised one arm in the air and waved it. "I'm done. I'm done," he called out in a tired, raspy voice.

The thin, denim overall clad referee rushed to the center of the ring and held up Anya's arm to the roar of the crowd. When he let go, Anya walked to the edge of the ring. When she was still several steps away from Jarrett, her knees buckled, and she went to the ground.

Cursing, he was by her side in an instant, scooping her up into his arms. He carried her to the wooden crates stacked against the wall where Pete had been perched when they arrived earlier in the evening. The massive owner of the fight club had been standing next to Jarrett when Anya collapsed and was now close on his heels.

"I'm fine," Anya protested from Jarrett's arms. "I'm fine."

Jarrett ignored her and laid her on the crates. She promptly sat up.

"I told you I'm fine," she groused.

"Yeah? So you were just inspecting the cleanliness of Pete's floor?" he asked.

"I had a twinge in my ankle."

"Your ankle? Which one?" he demanded, his hands automatically running over her legs.

"Left," she said lifting it up slightly, and Jarrett saw the grimace she tried to hide.

He unlaced her boot and gently pulled it off, followed by the sock. Anya hissed.

"Okay, a little more than a twinge," she admitted when he gave her a hard look.

He pushed her pant leg up to reveal a large expanse of swelling, blue-tinged skin.

"Here, let me take a look," Pete said.

Jarrett gave a start. He'd forgotten the man was next to him and turned to look at Pete with his huge, beefy hands. No way was he touching Anya.

Pete obviously read the thoughts on Jarrett's face because he gave a deep, hearty laugh. "I won't hurt her, boy. I'm a med-mage. Low level, to be sure, and I can't heal a paper cut, but I'm excellent at diagnostics. We need to see if her leg or ankle is broken."

"It's okay," Anya said, putting her hand on Jarrett's where it rested protectively on her knee.

Reluctantly Jarrett stepped aside and let Pete work. Pete rubbed his hands together for a long moment, holding them over Anya's ankle before he finally touched her, lifting her leg until it was straight out. A dark, raw jealousy clawed at Jarrett's stomach as he watched Pete's hands slide down the bare skin of her calf to her ankle.

He knew it was ridiculous, and not just because

the man was at least three decades older than Anya. Jarrett's jealousy was completely bonkers because Anya was in no way his property or possession to claim. Other men had touched her before, and in less than two weeks he'd be long gone from here, leaving her free to be touched by any other man she chose.

The thought elicited a rough growl from his throat.

"I'm okay," Anya said, patting his arm. She'd obviously mistook his sound as one of concern. He didn't correct her.

Pete sighed. "You are, but your ankle isn't. Nothing seems to be broken, but there are some torn muscles."

"Torn?" Jarrett asked, trying not to let his alarm show in his voice. That didn't sound good. He'd torn muscles before, and broken bones, but he was a vampire. He healed within hours and as long as the injury had been set properly, he had no lasting effects. But Anya was norm. A torn muscle for her could be disastrous, couldn't it?

"Don't look so stricken, both of you," Pete said. "A torn muscle is serious, but it's not anything to really be concerned about as long as you can get to a healer capable of deep healing. You'll want to find someone within the next twenty-four hours."

"We'll go right now," Jarrett said, not giving Anya a chance to speak.

Pete pulled Anya's pant leg down and eased her

sock on her foot while Anya grimaced and bit back a moan of pain. "Don't put the boot back on. Oh, and Jarrett, have them do a full body diagnostic on her. The healer will automatically heal that nasty cut above her eye, but I'm not convinced she fell because of her leg. A concussion could cause dizziness."

"When I'm on both feet I'm going to remember you two talking like I'm not even here, and kick both your asses. And I wasn't dizzy. It was my leg," she groused.

"Don't you get lippy with me, young lady," Pete growled. "I'm telling him what to do because he's going to see to it that you are well taken care of, or he'll answer to me."

Anya rolled her eyes. "Yeah, whatever you say Pete." There was a smile in her voice, and she leaned over and kissed the older man on his cheek.

Pete flashed a wide grin before carefully schooling his face back into a scowl. "Go on you two. I've got to get back to work. I've got a fight house to run, you know. Can't be playing healer all night." He turned and walked back to the crowd around the ring, as Anya and Jarrett laughed.

Once he was gone, Anya looked up at Jarrett. "Just take me to River; she'll know what to do."

Jarrett scooped her up. "You're going to the hospital. You heard what Pete said, you need a healer experienced in deep healing. I know River has some healing talent, but I don't think she can do what you need." He shifted her weight against him so that she was cradled comfortably in his arms as he strode out of the warehouse. "Besides, no way am I walking into Pinky's with you lying in my arms covered with blood. I wouldn't live long enough for you to tell him I didn't do this to you. Not that it would matter. He'd hold me responsible just for being in the room with you."

Anya screwed up her face in agreement. "Yeah, there's that." She sighed in defeat and laid her head against his shoulder. "Okay, take me to the hospital."

NINE
Jarrett

JARRETT EXPECTED ANYA TO PROTEST HIM CARRYING her all the way to a healer but she didn't. She'd only asked once, when they'd started across the bridge to the other side of the river, why he hadn't hired a rickshaw. She'd accepted his explanation without argument that carrying her would be faster because he wouldn't get caught in traffic, and it would jostle her ankle less and cause her less pain. To Jarrett's mind, her acceptance was a sign of just how much pain she was in. Anya wasn't nearly as cantankerous as Fiona, but like her sister, she didn't like giving up control. Though they hadn't known each other long, he knew her well enough to know that under normal circumstances, she wouldn't allow herself to be carried across the street, much less across town.

In an effort to get her healed as quickly as possible, he jogged across the bridge, careful to keep her ankle from bumping his body, and all the way to the clinic. It wasn't until Anya opened her eyes and saw where they were that she gave protest.

"Jarrett, this is City Hospital. You can't bring me here. They only treat employees of the city-state or Blades. I'm neither, so they won't treat me. There's a public clinic further down Broadway."

He didn't trust her health and her ability to walk on the chance that the med-mage at the public clinic had enough power and skill to take care of her properly. Though the healer's guild had high standards in the med-mages they certified to work in the clinics around the city-state, the fact was not all healers were created equal. They had different levels of power, and though every clinic was supposed to have at least one high-level med-mage on staff, there was no guarantee they would be on shift at the clinic. And, the city's public clinics usually worked with a minimal staff. City Hospital, located directly across the street from the Blade Headquarters, was the only place he knew of that was guaranteed to have several high-level med-mages on shift at all times.

"There's no guarantee there is a healer qualified to

help you at the other clinic, but there is here. Don't worry, they'll treat you. You may not be a Blade, but I am," he said, giving her a wink. Then he tilted his head and grinned. "As a matter of fact, not to brag or anything, I'm a pretty high-ranking member of one of the most elite special squads in the Blades. They'll treat you."

"But..."

"No buts, you'll see a med-mage, the highest ranking I can find, and you'll hush about it." He signaled the end of the conversation by shifting her weight against him so he could use one hand to push open the door.

He stepped into a small, sterile-looking lobby with a large desk in the center. The young man at the desk idly looked up as they walked in, and then jumped up. "How can I help you? Do I need to call an emergency team down?"

Jarrett would have laughed at the young man's flustered reaction if he hadn't understood it so well. In the short time it had taken him to get across the river and the few short blocks to the clinic, the bruises that covered Anya had turned from blue-tinged to deep purple. The cut above her left eye had continued to bleed so that blood streaked down her face and soaked her shirt. She had more blood smeared from the right corner of her mouth down her chin from a lucky punch landed by the opponent in her second fight.

"It's okay," Anya answered the young attendant, her voice soothing. "It looks worse than it is. I just need to see a med-mage if possible."

The attendant smiled at her. "Absolutely. I'll just need to see your credentials."

Before Jarrett could respond by showing his Kukri tattoo, Anya said, "I don't have any."

The attendant shook his head. "I'm so sorry, I can't help you. We have a strict policy. If it were life or death I could overlook it, but…"

"I have credentials," Jarrett growled, annoyed.

He shifted Anya's weight again so that he could push his right wrist out to the man. Both the attendant and Anya looked down. It was, of course bare. But Jarrett opened his senses and pushed a little power through his body, focusing on his wrist. Within seconds a black-lined tattoo appeared on his skin. The fleur-de-lis over crossed swords proved he was a Black Blade Guard agent, the curved blades of the swords denoted his position in the Kukri division.

"I'm Agent Jarrett Campbell, Kukri division, and I am authorizing treatment of this civilian," he said, his voice polite, but firm. "I wish to see the highest ranking med-mage on duty, please."

The young attendant nodded. "Yes sir. Go through this door, take the first hall on the left, then the second hall on the right and the trauma room is at the end of that hall. I'll scry back and let the healers know you are on your way."

"Thank you," Anya called back to the attendant as Jarrett carried her through the door behind the desk.

"Should have just walked around the building to the trauma entrance to start with. It would have gotten us in quicker," Jarrett mumbled under his breath.

Anya shook her head. "Give the boy a break. He was just doing his job. Speaking of jobs, why is your Blade tattoo invisible?"

Jarrett stopped for a moment, mid-stride and stared down at her. "Three words. Covert. Spy. Assassin."

Anya stared at him blankly for a moment, and then closed her eyes, shaking her head. "Oh, yeah."

Resuming their journey down the maze of halls, Jarrett explained, "There are several covert divisions of the Black Blade Guard. All those agents have ID tattoos that are specially spelled so that they appear only if the agent pulses energy through them with the intent to show them, or in case of the agent's death."

"That makes sense. I had never thought about it. I guess any time an agent goes undercover they get the same spell on their tat?"

"Yeah," Jarrett nodded. "But for regular agents that have to identify themselves on a regular basis, it's a nuisance, so they don't use it. And it looks like we are here." He indicated a set of double doors a few yards away.

Anya let out a sigh and wiggled uncomfortably in his arms. "Yay. I'm getting a little tired of being hauled around."

Jarrett, on the other hand, wasn't the least bit tired of holding her close. Vampiric strength and stamina came in handy sometimes. He was eager to get her healed. Though he knew the bruises and blood looked worse than what they were, he didn't like seeing her in pain. He was also a little anxious about the muscles in her leg. A few minutes, or even hours, probably wouldn't make a difference in whether or not her leg could be healed thoroughly and properly, but he didn't want to take any chances.

He pushed through the double doors into a large room with a circular desk in the center and narrow beds separated by curtains lining three of the walls. A tall, dark-skinned man looked up from where he stood near the desk and started towards them.

"Can I help y…Anya? What happened?" Then dark fury flashed in his eyes as he moved his gaze to Jarrett. "What did you do to her?"

"Don't be a pratt, Luca," Anya said from Jarrett's arms. "He didn't do anything to me. I was at Pete's Fight House. I had a match with a dude the size of a building. I won."

Luca stared at her a long moment, then, ignoring

her quirky smile as she said the last word, he shot a dagger stare at Jarrett. "You let her go up against an opponent that big? What were you thinking?"

If Jarrett hadn't thought the same thing a hundred times over the last half hour, he would have punched Luca in the mouth. Instead he said, "Since you know her name, I'm assuming you've met her. So I'm going to give you a moment to mull over how idiotic that question is."

Luca glared at him. "Fair enough. Sorry Anya, I didn't mean to imply you didn't make your own decisions."

"Yeah, I know. Look, I know I'm not actually authorized to get treatment here, but…"

Luca shook his head. "Don't worry about it. I run the place, so I get to decide who is authorized. I'll take care of you myself."

Jarrett said, "If you don't mind, I'd like her to be treated by the highest level med-mage on duty."

Luca shot him a withering look. "That's me. I'm the highest ranking med-mage in Nash. Now if you'll let me take her, we can get started." He held out his arms.

Unconsciously Jarrett pulled Anya tighter and took a step back. "I'll carry her wherever you need."

"That really isn't necessary." Luca's voice had a hard edge.

Jarrett assessed the other vampire. He was tall, but still a few inches shorter than Jarrett, broad shouldered and muscular. He could possibly be a force to be reckoned with, but Jarrett bet the man had never had any hand-to-hand combat training. He was, after all, just a doctor. If push came to shove, Jarrett was confident he could take the med-mage.

"Yes, I really think it is," Jarrett said, his tone brooking no argument.

"Seriously, you two, all this testosterone flying around has me giddy with excitement, but do you think you could put a cork in it. My leg hurts like a bitch and I'd like to get it healed so I can walk out of here before the two of you pull out a measuring stick," Anya groused.

"Sorry," they said in unison, and Jarrett felt like a heel. But he still wasn't handing her over.

Luca sighed. "Follow me."

Jarrett followed Luca to one of the narrow beds and laid Anya down on it.

"Thank you," Luca said. "You can wait over there." He pointed to a couple of chairs near one wall.

Jarrett walked behind the bed, crossed his arms, and leaned against the wall. "I'll stay, thanks."

Anya looked at him and rolled her eyes, clearly indicating she thought he was acting like a child. But, she turned to Luca and said, "It's okay, he can stay."

"Okay," the med-mage said, obviously unhappy with the situation. He pulled the curtain around them so they had a modicum of privacy.

"Pete checked my leg and said there was a torn muscle, but he advised I have a full diagnostic," Anya said.

"Okay. Let me check you out first, then we'll get you healed," Luca told her, his voice tender.

As Jarrett watched, the other man ran his hands over Anya, making notes on a pad of hemp paper. Although it was all very clinical, Jarrett felt like the jealousy raging through him was much more justified now than it had been with Pete. He didn't know how well Anya and the med-mage knew each other, but it was clear Luca had feelings for her that were more than just friendly.

But then, Jarrett really couldn't justify his jealousy, could he? Anya wasn't his. If this man wanted Anya, it was her problem, not Jarrett's. He still didn't like it. But most of all, he didn't like feeling like this. He hadn't felt jealous or possessive of a woman in centuries. And now wasn't the time to feel it again. Not with this woman.

Even if he did want to be with someone for more than a few days at a time, it couldn't be Anya. She was a norm, he was a vampire. She would grow old and die in just a blink of his eye. He had absolutely no business getting attached to her. Yet as he stood there and watched her talking to the med-mage, Jarrett knew it was too late. He was already attached. All he could do at this point was go with it, and once he left Nash, make sure his work didn't bring him back for a decade or two.

"Pete was right in his assessment," Luca said, breaking Jarrett out of his musings. "You do have a torn muscle, but I can heal it with no problem. You don't have a concussion and your other injuries are minor. I'm going to have one of the other healers work on your cuts and bruises so I can focus on your leg, is that okay?"

"Sure. Thank you," Anya said, smiling up at him.

Luca stepped beyond the curtain for a moment, then was back, a female healer following him.

Jarrett's abilities to manipulate energy were minimal, and he couldn't normally sense when magic was being used like some high-level mages could, yet as the two med-mages worked on Anya, he could feel palpable shifts of energy inside the tiny cubicle.

The woman first rubbed a salve over Anya's cuts, and Jarrett assumed it was to clean and disinfect them. Then, she placed her hands over each cut and bruise, one by one, and pushed power through her hands. When she lifted her hands away, the bruise was gone.

"It's good that you got here so quickly," the female healer said after removing the first, darkest bruise. "I'll be able to heal these completely. The deepest bruises might have a slight yellowish tinge for a few hours, but all discoloration should be faded by morning. There shouldn't be any pain at all. If you had waited, that would not have been the case. Once a bruise is a few hours old, it becomes more difficult to heal."

Anya turned her head and looked at him. He flashed a grin and a wink that clearly said 'I told you so.' Translating it well, she stuck her tongue out at him and turned back to pay attention to the healers.

While the woman healed the smaller injuries, Luca worked on Anya's leg. He placed his hands over it and seemed to be pushing bursts of energy through his hands as he moved them up and down. After about half an hour, he pulled his hands away to reveal Anya's ankle. It was back to its normal color and size.

"Okay, Baby Girl, you are all done," Luca said, pulling her pants leg down and flashing her a flirty smile that made Jarrett's urge to punch him in the teeth come back with a vengeance. "It's healed and the pain should be gone, but that was a fairly serious tear, so the muscle will be weak for a little while. I want you to stay off it for about twelve hours. After that, you be back to normal. We can put you in a room here until you feel you can walk back to the pub tomorrow."

Jarrett pushed away from the wall. "I'll take her home."

Luca didn't look at Jarrett. "You'll need to stay off your leg, completely. That means you'll need someone to help you to the restroom and bring you food and drink. You're better off here with the nurses than at home where everyone is busy working."

Jarrett pushed away from the wall. "I'll be taking care of her, no need to worry."

Anya looked up and smiled at him and his heart leapt in his chest when she took his hand in hers. "It's okay, Luca, Jarrett will make sure I stay off my foot and am well taken care of."

"Well, okay then," he turned to go, and then turned back. "You were right to come here tonight."

She crinkled her nose. "To be honest, if Jarrett hadn't insisted I come here, I would have gone to the public clinic down the road."

Horror flashed across his face. "I'm glad you didn't. I know which one you are talking about. There are very talented healers there, but none that can do deep healing. You would have been sent across town. That kind of delay would have made the healing take longer and be more painful. You would have likely been on crutches for several days, if not weeks. Look, Sweetness, if you ever need healing again, come here and ask for me. If I'm not here, have me called in."

She smiled up at him. "Thank you, Luca. That is so kind."

"Anything for you, Baby Girl. I have to keep my favorite bartender able to pour drinks and listen to my whining." He walked over to her, bent to drop a kiss on her forehead, and then left the tiny cubicle. Jarrett stared after him, fists clenched at his side.

TEN
Jarrett

AFTER LEAVING THE CLINIC, JARRETT CARRIED ANYA back to his boat, and then went out to get them some food. After they ate the fish tacos he'd purchased from a vendor's stand on the dock, he helped her shower away the dirt, sweat, and blood. Then they settled into bed.

They lay there for what seemed like a long time. To Jarrett, lying with Anya snuggled into his arms, neither of them asleep or talking, just quietly being together, felt more intimate than making love. It was something he'd never experienced before, and he didn't dislike it. But, after a while, the question that had been burning all night at the back of his mind made him break the sweet, peaceful silence.

"Why do you fight?" he asked, his hand lazily stroking her arm.

She shrugged. "I don't know, I guess because it's a waste of my training not to. You know Fiona got Sam to pull strings so that I could go to the Academy of Magic and Science with her."

"I knew you attended, but I didn't know that."

Anya sat up, pulling the sheet with her and wrapping it around her torso to cover her breasts, much to Jarrett's consternation. She sat cross-legged next to him on the bed.

"Fiona started at the Academy at fourteen under a City-Guard contract, and because of her power and skill, went straight into the Blades. But I'm a norm, I couldn't sign a guard contract and there were no guilds to contract with."

Jarrett nodded. To him, the Academy was a new-fangled way of training city guards and Blades, but he understood how it worked. Originally built to teach and train the Black Blade Guard agents and City Guard officers, the cadets signed contracts to work at least two years in exchange for their free education and training. It had opened almost half a century ago to civilians, and now the rich could pay for their children to learn math, history, science, and magic beyond what they could learn at home or in community-run schools. But few could afford the tuition. Many mages were able to attend by signing contracts with local trade guilds. Depending upon their type and level of magic, they could contract with an organization like the crystal chargers guild, the healer's guild, or any of a dozen other trade guilds, to work for the guild or in a guild-run shop for two years for a minimum wage and the cost of their education. There were no such trade guilds or scholarship contracts available for norms.

"Pinky couldn't afford to send me," Anya went on. "But Fiona wouldn't take no for an answer. And you know how she is. Just before she started her second year at the Academy, she threw a hissy fit and threatened to quit if I couldn't go."

Jarrett chuckled. "That doesn't surprise me. I'm guessing she threw the fit in the middle of Sam's office."

Anya nodded, smiling at the memory. "Yep. Sam has always been like an uncle to all of us, and you know he can't say no to Fiona. So, he pulled some strings and I got in. Of course, all I'd ever wanted to be was a Black Blade Guard, like I knew Fiona was going to be, so that's the curriculum track I went on. I took physical training, law and administration classes, everything. But then the two years of school were done, and it was time to test and become an official guard cadet. I was allowed to take the test because it was a part of the graduation requirements, but despite the fact that I had the highest grades in the class, I was denied cadet status."

"Because you're a norm." Jarret said.

She nodded. "Got it in one. They told me it was too dangerous of a job for a norm. I had always known that was the policy, but I'd ignored it. I guess I thought that Fiona's temper had gotten me in the door, but my skill and determination would get me to where I really wanted to be. And I really wanted to be a guard. But it was a no-go. I was offered a job in administration. I could work at the City-Guard offices, or even in the Black Blade Guard offices, but I could never be an officer or an agent."

"That really sucks." He felt stupid because that was all he could think to say.

"You said it. It sucks." She gave a half laugh. "Could you see me sitting behind a desk typing up reports all day? I'd have kicked someone in the throat two hours into my first shift just to relieve the boredom."

"I could definitely see that as a potential outcome," Jarrett said through laughter. "If it means anything, I think tending bar suits your personality more than administrative work ever could. Though I can see where you would want to do something more physical once in a while."

"I started out just training with Fiona on the weekends when she was going through her year of Blade training. Then I started street-fighting for the money. Now, I still make a pretty good side income through the fight houses I frequent, but it's more about the physical activity, and maybe a little about the adrenaline rush."

"Nope, sorry, don't buy it," Jarrett said.

"Excuse me?" Anya said, sounding more than a little put off.

"I get that those are the reasons why you fight, to a point. But I think there is more to the story. Your frustration at not being able to work in your chosen field is enough to make you want to show off your skill every chance you get. But it won't make you fight like a demon's after you," he said.

"I don't know what you mean," she replied, shaking her head, her brow furrowed.

"When you fight, you aren't just fighting to show your skill. You are driven by something deeper, darker. I saw it a little in your first two fights, but nothing like that last one. After he knocked you down, you fought with a rage and fury that could only be fueled by deep, dark pain. And not the kind in your leg."

"I..." she mumbled, a shadow moving across her features.

"Don't deny it. I saw it." He kept his voice low and gentle. "I know it's not my business, but will you tell me what it is? Will you tell me what makes you fight so ferociously?"

She let out a tiny, sad laugh. "You know, you're the first person to ever ask me. Well, my family knows, but no one else has ever paid enough attention or cared enough to ask."

He took her hand in his. "You don't have to answer. You can tell me to shut the hell up and mind my own business, but I hope you won't. I'd like to know what caused you so much pain."

She let out another laugh, and this one had a little more spunk in it than the first. "Why, so you can go kick its ass?"

He flashed his most toothy grin at her. "Maybe."

Her smile had a sad tinge to it. "Somehow I have no doubt that you would if you could, but there's nothing for you to assassinate. It's just bad, old memories. But I'll tell you, on one condition."

One eyebrow shot up. "What's that?" he asked, dubious.

"Let's lie back down, and you can hold me while I tell you my story."

"Okay," he said softly.

They laid down on the bed, both on their sides, her back against his chest and his arms around her. They lay quietly like that for a long moment, but Jarrett didn't want to push her. He had a feeling that whatever she was going to tell him was very painful for her to even think about. After a while, she began to speak.

"I know you're older than Pinky, so that means you grew up in a world where most people had no idea magic existed."

It wasn't exactly a question, but Jarrett answered anyway. "I did. As a matter of fact, the world I grew up in considered magic an abomination. Magic and paranormal creatures were believed to be nothing more than stuff of fairy tales. Yet any talk of real magic was considered evil, an abomination. I had a hard time adjusting to the truth when I was changed. It took a long time to realize that I, and those around me, weren't inherently evil because of what we had become."

"Then you might understand this better than I thought. You grew up with fairy tales of magic. I grew up in a world of magic where the fairy tales I told myself at night were of a world where magic didn't exist. I spent the first decade of my life wishing for such a world, or just one tiny place in it."

Though he was positive he wasn't going to like the answer, Jarrett asked, "Why?"

"I grew up in a gypsy clan. According to the few stories that existed, my ancestors fled their homes during the cataclysm, and like many families, never found a place to call home. After a couple of generations, traveling was home. It was the one thing I ever enjoyed about my childhood, moving around, meeting new people."

Jarrett dropped a kiss on the top of her head and

smiled into her hair. "Something we have in common. I've been a nomad all my life. First by the fate of birth, then by choice."

She turned her head slightly to look at him, "Really? I'd like to hear about it."

He kissed her again, this time on the tip of her nose. "Nice try. Some other time. Right now is time for your story."

She stuck her tongue out at him, and then flipped to face him so that her head rested against his chest. "Well, as I said, I was born into a gypsy family, which isn't such a bad thing. But, fate is a fickle bitch and didn't seem to be in my favor. I was born a norm in a family of mages. Mages that used their powers to make money, both legally and illegally."

Jarrett didn't like where this was going, but he remained silent.

"I don't really remember what it was like before my parents realized I was norm. But once they did, they weren't happy."

"But you still were quite young when you came to live with Pinky, weren't you? Magic abilities don't usually present until puberty," Jarrett cut in.

Anya shook her head against his chest. "That is when they are measurable, and specific abilities become apparent. Most magic users have the ability to manipulate energy at least on very low levels at a young age. I don't know exactly how old I was, around four or five, but I remember not being able to turn off a crystal lantern, and one of my cousins, who was the same age, turned it off for me. An adult noticed and they made me try over and over again for hours to turn it on. I couldn't. That's when they realized I was a norm, or dud, as they called me."

Jarrett didn't want to remark on the word 'dud' so instead he said, "But I've seen you turn crystal lanterns on and off."

She rolled over to face him. "Of course I can now. Like you said, puberty. Even norms that rank with 10% or less brain usage can activate crystals charged with basic household spells, just like you can, even though your magic is limited. It's not about being able to push energy. Those crystals are activated by the basic electromagnetic energy in our bodies, which gets more powerful after puberty. Norm children can't use charged crystals."

Jarrett's brow furrowed. "I didn't know that."

Anya laughed. "I guess it is possible to learn something new, even when you're older than dirt." She laughed harder at his faux-offended expression. "But I only know because I am a norm, and I made it a point to learn what I could, after Pinky rescued me, of course."

Jarrett felt his smile fade. "He rescued you?"

Anya's expression shaded, all humor gone. "He did. As I said, my parents weren't happy about my 'dud' status. I was considered useless because I wasn't able to do anything to earn my keep. And not just by my family, but by all the families in the clan. I was relegated to nothing more than animal status, lower actually, because at least the dogs aided in hunting and security. All I could do was scrub pots and wagon floors. The fact that I couldn't even use magic for those menial tasks made them even angrier at me."

A sharp pain jabbed into Jarrett's chest. How awful for her, to feel so unwanted as a child. His own childhood perhaps hadn't been ideal, but for the short time that he had his father, Jarrett had known the man loved and wanted him. He lifted a hand up to caress her cheek, but she brushed it away.

"Let me finish. If you're too sweet I won't be able to finish the story, and now that I've started, I need to tell you all of it," she said, her eyes down, her voice tremulous.

He pulled his hand back. "Okay, I'm listening."

"I was beaten for every tiny infraction. Since I couldn't seem to do anything fast enough or right, that meant I was beaten for everything I did. A day never went by, from the time I was around four or five, that I wasn't beaten for something. Most days, the only time I wasn't dodging slaps or even getting spit on by the other clan members was when I was hiding out in whatever woods we were camped in or asleep on my pallet under my family's wagon."

Pain thumped in Jarrett's chest, and rage stormed through him. How could anyone treat any child like that, much less their own? He wanted nothing more than to find her parents and rip their heads from their bodies. But he did his best to keep his breath steady and not show his emotions to Anya. Her voice was quiet and shaky, but she wasn't crying. He had a feeling that any show of anger or negative emotion from him would change that.

After pausing a moment, Anya took a deep breath and kept going.

"In the eyes of my clan, I was completely worthless, and they took pride in telling me so. The other children made a game out of teasing, taunting, and hitting me. If I hit back, they would gang up on me and hold me down. I had no friends, no allies, no one that cared an inch about me. But that all changed the day I met Pinky, Fiona, and River." She looked up at him with watery eyes, a small, tremulous smile trying to take hold on her lips.

He smiled back at her. "Tell me about that."

"I don't know exactly how old I was, since after it was discovered I had no magic, my birthdays weren't celebrated anymore. But I tried to guess when it was time for it to come around, so I was around seven and a half. We were in Nash for market week. I was carrying a pot of stew from the fire to the table for lunch. It was hot and heavy, and I stumbled on a rock and fell. I dropped the stew and it spilled all over the ground."

Her voice was far away, as if she were back in that moment. Jarrett stayed silent and listened.

"My mother was furious. She grabbed a horsewhip that was hanging on one of the wagons and started whipping me. She only landed one blow. I was braced for the next, but it never came. I looked up and this tall, thin man in a dark, billowing cloak had the whip wrapped around his hand and my mother was kneeling on the ground next to me."

"Pinky," Jarrett whispered, but he didn't know why.

"Yes. His blue eyes were glowing, but I wasn't scared. He held my mother in a trance, and asked her questions, forcing her to answer truthfully. Then he asked me my name, my age, and other questions. He asked me if I was happy living there and if I got whipped often. I told him the truth. He told my mother that the city guard knew of their illegal activities and would be there soon. Then he told her that they should leave Appalachia on the next barge out of port and never return or they would be arrested, and that she had turned me over to an orphanage and was well rid of me."

"Wow, that's some power," Jarrett said, more than a

little impressed.

Anya nodded. "It was impressive to behold, a little scary, too. Though I was never actually scared of him. My mother started screaming to everyone else to start packing up and Pinky told me to get my things. I didn't have anything to get, so he took my hand and led me out. On the way out of the market, he stopped and had me tell a city guard what I knew of my clan's illegal activities, and then he took me home. There was never even a suggestion of taking me to an orphanage. Just like that, I had a home and a family. A father and sisters."

Jarrett lifted his hand and brushed a tear off her cheek with his thumb. "I'm so sorry you had to go through that. I'm glad Pinky saved you. Remind me to thank him the next time I see him."

She turned her head to kiss the palm of his hand. "You'll have to thank River, too. She was only around four. She'd had a vision, and though she was too young to be able to articulate why it was important, she threw a temper tantrum until Pinky agreed to go to the market that day, in the middle of the morning when the sun was high."

"No wonder you and Fiona dote on her."

"Yeah, she's a treasure," Anya said, her smile brightening before a thoughtful look slid into place. "To answer your original question, I guess I fight because it makes me feel in control. It helps me assure myself I'll never be a victim again."

"You are an amazing fighter. I've always admired Fiona's fighting moves, but you surpass her. You move with precision and grace."

"So you aren't going to lecture me about taking on a guy four times my size and getting seriously injured?"

After seeing her bruised and bloodied, Jarrett wanted to forbid her from ever stepping into a ring again, but he had no control over what she did. Nor did he have any right to want to control her, as if she ever could be controlled by him or anyone. "I'm pretty sure he was closer to five times your size. And no, it wasn't very smart to get in the ring with him after you'd already fought two opponents." He grinned at her. "But even with your injury, you did put him down. That was pretty awesome."

A light shined in her eyes at his praise. "Thanks. How about I make you a deal. You don't tell my family about me getting hurt tonight, and I'll promise to be smarter in taking fights."

Jarrett rolled his eyes. "I think you'll keep doing whatever you want to do, no matter what I say. But I won't tell your family. Unless they ask straight out, because they haven't yet found the body of the last person who lied to Fiona."

She laughed. "Fair enough. I just don't want them to worry more than they already do."

"They love you."

"Yeah, they really do. I was lucky they found me."

He put a finger under her chin and lifted her face to his so their eyes met. "And they are lucky to have found you."

She flashed him a quick, toothy smile. "Of course they are. I'm fabulous." She was quiet a moment before continuing, "You know, I've never told anyone about my childhood before. My family knows, of course, but after I got settled in, we never talked about it again. You know, I thought it would be much more painful to talk about than it was."

"I didn't want to hurt you by asking," he told her.

"You didn't. I think I hadn't talked about it before because no one ever asked. I'm actually glad you did. Now I know I can talk about it, think about it, without crumbling into a hysterical wreck. I actually feel good after telling you."

"I'm glad."

"I know what will make me feel even better," she said.

"What?"

She leaned up and pressed her mouth to his in a long, hot kiss. She was smiling seductively when she leaned back. "Make love to me."

His whole body went hot and hard. "Oh, I can definitely do that."

And he did, slowly and tenderly, until they fell asleep in each other's arms.

ELEVEN
Anya

IT WAS MID-AFTERNOON THE NEXT DAY BEFORE I COULD drag myself out of bed. Not because I was still hurt, Luca and the other healer had done an excellent job. There were no signs of any cuts or bruises, and my ankle felt good as new. My weariness had nothing to do with my injuries and everything to do with the fact that Jarrett and I had made love all night, finally drifting off to sleep just after dawn.

After the talk we'd had, I'd been emotionally raw and needed his touch in a way I had never before needed anyone's touch. Luckily, after I assured him again that Luca's healing had taken away my physical pain, he'd been more than happy to oblige.

It had been an impassioned night. I stood in the

head—it felt weird to call the bathroom that—brushing my hair, and I looked through the doorway to where he sat on the edge of his bed pulling on his boots. He was shirtless and the way his muscles flexed as he moved made me want to crawl back in the bed with him. But I couldn't. I'd promised River I'd pick up meat and blood from the butcher on my way home to help her with tonight's family dinner.

I groaned silently. Well, that thought took all the lingering sensual feelings right out of me. I'd almost forgotten about tonight's family dinner and the fact that Pinky had invited Jarrett the night before last.

"Are you sure you want to come tonight?"

Jarrett looked up at me, his expression blank. "Anya, that is the third time you've asked me that since Pinky invited me. Are you sure you want me to come?"

I sighed. "I do, I just don't want you to feel pressured or obligated."

"I don't. Pinky asked me to dinner, I said yes. No pressure."

I laughed at his naivety. "Of course there was no pressure during the invitation. That will come later, during dinner. Pinky has never invited someone I was dating to dinner before. I want to think he invited you because you are now a friend of the family. But I can't promise things won't get weird."

It was Jarrett's turn to laugh. "Do you think he's

going to ask what my intentions are towards his precious daughter?"

"He won't if he knows what's good for him," I quipped. "But I never know what the heck Pinky might do. I just don't want you to feel like you're being inspected by the family or that you have to go just to be nice or something."

"Anya, who are you afraid will think there is more to our relationship than there is? Your family, me, or you?" he asked, coming up behind me, slipping his arms around me, and dropping a kiss on my neck.

I turned in his arms and leaned back so that I could look up into his face. I had no idea how to answer his question, so I avoided it. "I just don't want you to think I am expecting more of you than what this thing between us actually is."

"And what is this thing between us?" He cocked his head to the side in a curious manner, but his eyes were unreadable.

"Hell if I know. It just is what it is, until your leave is up and it isn't anymore. I don't want you to think because I invited you to a family dinner I expect anything more than that."

He laughed. The damned man actually laughed at me. "Well, you didn't invite me to dinner. Pinky did. Besides, I've had dinner with your family before."

"Yeah, but they didn't see you as my 'date' then.

They may be a little nuttier than usual."

"It's not a problem. I actually like spending time with your family. I've never really spent time in a real family setting before."

"You mean other than your own," I said, curious.

"I didn't exactly have a traditional family." He chuckled.

I couldn't help the peel of laughter I let out.

"Couldn't be more untraditional than mine. My sisters and I all come from different backgrounds and were adopted by a vampire who was changed so young that he now looks like he could be our younger brother."

"Yeah, well, my mother was from a tribe of natives who'd never seen a white man before. My father was a sailor on a ship that got damaged during a storm. They took refuge on my mother's island. She died in childbirth and I grew up on sailing ships. The only family I ever had were sailors. Well, to be completely truthful, pirates. My family was a bunch of foul-mouthed, plundering, and pillaging pirates," he said, grinning down at me.

"Okay, you win," I laughed. "Your family was definitely more untraditional than mine. On the plus side, though, since you grew up with pirates and cutthroats, a dinner with my family will be a piece of cake."

"So, you aren't worried anymore?"

"No," I said, looking away so he couldn't see my lie.

"Good, so I'll see you this evening around seven," he said, pulling away and leaving me to finish putting my hair up on my head in a loose bun.

"Yeah, that sounds good."

I gathered my things, gave him another long kiss that promised sexy and sensual things later, and left the boat. The walk home gave me more time than I wanted to think about our conversation and my feelings in general.

The truth was, I'd never been worried about how he would deal with my family. They liked him already, and over the past few nights he'd been around all of them quite a bit. Added to that, Fiona was his best friend. No worries. What had my stomach all in knots had nothing to do with my family.

I wasn't even that worried about what he thought about my intentions towards him. He would think what he would think. I couldn't control that. Any more than, it seemed, I could control my own feelings.

Having Jarrett come to our weekly family dinner was disconcerting me because of how much I wanted him there. In the past, I'd never wanted anyone I dated to spend time with me around my family. I wanted it now, and that had me more than a little freaked out.

I was getting way too attached to Jarrett. His leave

would end next week and he'd sail off to parts unknown. Who knew when he'd return to Nash City, if at all in my lifetime. And that was fine, or it should be. I knew from the start that was how it would be. But I found myself missing him at night while I was working, and I got a little thrill every morning when he walked into the bar to have a drink before walking me back to his boat for a morning of lovemaking. I fell for him a little more each day. And then last night happened. I'd never opened myself up to anyone like that before.

Until now, I'd never experienced heartache because of a lover. With every passing day with Jarrett, no, every passing minute, I knew I was hurtling towards just that. But somehow, I couldn't give up the giddy happiness being around him gave me, even though I had a feeling it was going to hurt like hell when he left.

Of all the men in the world that could have been the one I'd get feelings for, why did it have to be a vampire? And not just any vampire. I had to form an attachment with a globe-trotting, ladies' man, assassin vampire who never stayed in one place longer than two weeks and probably had a woman in every port. Even if he did have feelings for me, it would never work out. He was a vampire, I was a norm. He traveled for his job, and mine kept me stuck in Nash.

There was no way around the facts. There was no way there could be any future for us. But that didn't mean I couldn't enjoy the present. Once he left, I'd deal with whatever consequences there were, but there wasn't any reason why I couldn't enjoy this new experience while it lasted. With my mind made up to stop worrying about where things were going and just let them take their own course, I felt better and looked forward to dinner with my family and Jarrett.

When we were young, we had dinner together as a family every night. As we grew up, went to school, and found our own jobs, instead of having family dinner every night or on weekends when Fiona and I were home from school, they came more and more sporadically, but never completely died out. Since Fiona had moved out, they were even rarer. Tonight was a special treat.

I stopped at the butcher shop as I'd promised River. Then, on a whim, I went in the bakery and bought some fresh baked bread and a cake for dessert. Back at home, I changed clothes, and then helped River and Farrah pull two tables together in the pub. We finished setting the table, and Fiona and Ian arrived just in time to help us bring the food down from our apartment where River had prepared it. With the addition of Farrah and Ian to our family, along with the inclusion of Jarrett, we had more people and food at our dinner table than ever before. River served up roasted lamb with potatoes, carrots, spinach, and fresh sliced tomatoes.

Along with the bread I'd purchased from the bakery, side dishes of blood for Pinky and Jarrett, and mugs of mead for all, it was a veritable feast.

Everyone chatted and joked as we ate. Even Farrah, who was often quiet and introverted, joined in the laughter and conversation. Everything was fine until River was serving the cake and a buzzing sounded.

"Fiona, is that your porta-scry? You know it's not allowed at the table during family night," Pinky said, disapprovingly.

"I know, sorry. I'm working a case. I'll be right back," she said hastily, pulling out the scry-crystal and going into kitchen for privacy.

She came out a few minutes later, tucking the porta-scry back into her pocket.

Pinky let out a much-put-upon sigh. "Are you going to have to rush out even before dessert?"

She stopped at his chair and kissed him on the cheek before going back to her own seat. "No, cranky pants, I don't have to leave. Not yet, anyway. I've got some time to kill, but I will have to leave after cake."

No one said anything else about Fiona's call and the meal resumed. Once the carrot cake had been decimated and nothing remained but crumbs, Fiona said, "That was delicious, Rivs. Pinky, I really am sorry, but I've got to run. I may not get another chance like the one that just fell in my lap."

Pinky sighed. "No problem, you go catch your bad guys. Be careful," he said, kissing her on the cheek before retreating into the kitchen with a stack of dirty dishes.

Ian said his goodbyes and left, after first kissing Fiona and giving her the same "Be careful" message as Pinky.

Jarrett and I were leaning against the bar when she came over to us. "So, you have any plans for the next couple of hours besides warming a barstool and watching my sister serve drinks?" she asked Jarrett.

He laughed. "I'm guessing I do now. You need some back up?"

"Nothing major, just some surveillance, but a little company never hurt. You don't mind, do you, An?"

I shook my head. "Nah. You two go have fun."

"It's not fun, An, it's work," Fiona protested.

I laughed and rolled my eyes. "For you it's the same thing. Both of you."

Jarrett nodded, and Fiona laughed and said, "You aren't wrong, sister. So, Jarrett, are you in?"

"Lead on, my friend," he said. Halfway to the door he stopped, came back and kissed me until my blood hummed. "I'll see you later," he whispered in my ear, turned, and followed Fiona out.

Once they were gone, River went up to the roof to work in her garden, Farrah and Pinky went in the kitchen to clean up the dinner dishes, and I started preparing to open the pub for the night's business. Shortly before opening time, the door swung open. I turned to tell whoever it was they'd have to come back and came face-to-face with a tall, muscular man with dark, creamy skin.

"Luca, hi," I greeted with a smile. "What are you doing here so early?"

"I just wanted to stop by and make sure your leg was doing okay. No pain or weakness?"

I hopped up and down on the leg in question. "Nope. It's as good as new."

"Why would your leg have pain and weakness?" Pinky's voice sounded from behind me.

Damn vampire hearing.

I sighed and Luca grimaced.

"Sorry," he said.

"It's okay," I said. Then I turned to Pinky and explained what had happened the night before. I hadn't wanted to tell him, but I wasn't going to lie now that he knew something was up.

I could see the silent fury in his eyes, but his voice was calm and steady when he asked Luca what the injury had been and how severe.

Luca explained about the tear and how he'd healed it. Then, at Pinky's insistence, he checked it out again, just to make sure it was healed completely and properly.

Once he'd pronounced my leg in perfect shape, he said he had to head to work and left.

The door swung shut behind him, and Pinky rounded on me.

"Damn it, Anya, we've discussed this." He slammed his hand down on the bar to punctuate his words, and I was surprised it didn't shatter. "I know you are a big girl and you can take care of yourself, but you take risks. Yes, you are an amazing fighter, but you are reckless. You were lucky it was just a torn muscle last night. One wrong move, one wrong twist or bad landing and you are either paralyzed or worse. You are strong, but your body is fragile. I wouldn't object to you participating in the fights at Pete's if you didn't take so many fool chances."

I stood there quietly for a long moment, letting him say his piece and let out his frustration, and then I said, "I know. You're right on every count. But you don't have to worry. I think I'm going to be fighting a lot less in the future."

He stared at me open mouthed. "You actually sounded like you meant that. Did you finally get hurt bad enough last night to scare you?"

"Actually, no," I answered truthfully. "After I was healed, Jarrett and I had a long talk about why I fight. And I told him about my life before you found me."

"I've never known you to talk about that with

anyone," Pinky said, his expression softening.

"I haven't. But doing so made me realize that I sometimes push boundaries when I'm fighting just to prove to myself that I can take care of myself no matter what. That no one will ever have the power to hurt me without me hurting them worse."

"Oh, sweetheart," Pinky said, his voice sad. "I always guessed it was something like that, but I had no idea how to make you see it. I just hoped you would come to it on your own."

I smiled at him. "I did, with Jarrett's help. And I know I've said this before, but I really mean it this time. I'm not going to promise to stop fighting, because, let's face it, I like it. It's fun. But I really will be smarter about the opponents I choose and stop taking crazy risks."

"If Jarrett got you to say all that and really mean it, I might need to give that man a kiss."

"Don't even think about it," I said, laughing.

He gave me a pleading look. "Not even a little peck? He looks like he'd be an excellent kisser."

"He is, and he's off limits," I said, unnecessarily. Pinky's sexual appetites might be fluid, but he never hit on a man that he didn't know would appreciate his advances, and he would never make a move on someone one of us was involved with.

He gave an over-blown sigh. "Oh, okay. I guess I'll

just have to do with a hug from my favorite middle daughter."

"Gladly," I said, letting him pull me into a warm, tight embrace.

After a long moment, he pulled away. "Okay, enough of that. We open the doors to the thirsty hordes in twenty minutes. Let's finish getting set up."

"Okay, boss," I said and went back to stacking glasses behind the bar.

TWELVE
Jarrett

"SO, WHAT'S THE PLAN?" JARRETT ASKED. He and Fiona had left Pinky's Pub and were strolling through the early evening crowd on Broadway towards the docks.

"We're going to have a couple of drinks," she told him.

He shot her a sideways look. "I'm going to take a wild guess that you didn't fake that call and aren't trying to sneak away from Ian for a few hours. And I know we aren't off to have an illicit tryst. So, care to let loose a little more info?"

"Wow, you're quick on your feet." She muttered a couple of words that Jarrett knew were a spell that would keep anyone near them from overhearing their conversation.

"As I said, surveillance. There's a new drug floating around. There have been two deaths in as many weeks. As far as we can tell it isn't wide spread, yet. I have an informant who bartends at a dive bar down by the docks. A friend told him he had a line on where he could get his hands on a top-notch high. And he knew the guy was looking for local dealers."

"Your informant is a dealer? I thought you guys were pretty good at keeping a lid on the illegal drug market inside the city."

"We are. He got busted for selling Juice a while back."

Jarrett made a face and shivered. "Uck. Shifter blood. That is nasty shit, but not illegal to use."

"No, but it's illegal to sell if it isn't your own blood. Mostly to deter people from kidnapping shifters and draining them dry," she said. "You know, you drink blood to live, how can you cringe at shifter blood?"

"Because, I got some by accident once. I was sick for a week. It might make mages and norms stronger and hyped up for a while, but it's the only thing I know of that can make a vampire vomit. I hadn't felt so bad since I had a stomach virus when I was a young boy." Jarrett said, the memory making him a little queasy.

"Anyway, my guy tells his buddy he's looking to make a little extra cash and asks if he can hook him up. When the buddy told him the distributor is giving away the first batch to new dealers, my guy knew something was off and called me."

"Giving away product isn't very profitable," Jarrett said. "I don't blame the guy for thinking something smelled funny. Why do you suppose someone is giving away free drugs?"

"Like I said, it's a dive. It caters to dock workers and sailors. Not exactly a sucker hangout, but bloodsucking and drug use is overlooked. If I were a drug manufacturer and wanted to test my product, somewhere like that would be the perfect laboratory."

"And apparently it's not the first testing field."

"No. Both deaths have been in similar bars around the city. The first one we didn't catch as a drug death. There were elements of vampire saliva in the blood, but no recent bite marks. The same thing was found in the second death, but this time the boy had never been bitten. No scars. And his friend said he drank a vial of something someone had given him a little while before he freaked out and started throwing chairs, and then had a heart attack. His friends didn't know who gave him the vial." Fiona said, keeping her voice low as they walked.

"A drug made with vampire saliva? Could that be possible?" Jarrett asked, incredulous.

She shook her head. "I don't know. That's one of the many things we need to find out. My informant, Carl, had his buddy set up a meeting with the distributor. He's supposed to get a sample of the goods to see if he wants to deal them in his bar."

"So no full deal going down? You can't arrest on a sample," Jarrett said.

She shot him a grin. "We aren't arresting, we're observing. The meet will go down in public, and then we'll trail the guy and see what we can find out. The main objective is getting a sample to analyze. If possible, trace the guy back to his base of operations. But the key is observation. We can't make any arrests until whatever he is selling can be analyzed and classified as an illegal drug. To do that, we have to connect that drug to the substance found in our two victims."

"Got it. So, we're just a couple out on the town?" He looked down at his clothes, and then over at Fiona's. They were dressed nearly identically in black leather pants and vests, and combat boots. The only difference was their shirts. "Are we going to be able to pull that off?"

"At the bar we're going to, yeah. But, just in case, let me make an adjustment," she said.

As they walked, she pulled the drawstring out of her tunic and tugged the fabric so that it fell down, baring the tops of her shoulders. With another tug, the material just barely peeked out of the top of her tight leather vest, revealing an ample amount of cleavage.

Then she took the ribbon out of the end of her braid and ran her fingers through her hair, shaking out the long, dark locks.

She stopped and turned to him, hands on her hips. "What do you think?"

He ran his gaze over her; she was definitely a knockout, even dressed to kick ass. With her hair wild and her cleavage popping out, she could make almost any man's mouth water. "I think if Ian could see you right now, he'd try to kick my ass."

She laughed. "I'll take that as a compliment," she said and resumed walking.

They walked over the bridge and to an area on the opposite side of the bridge from the market and Pete's Fight House. The area was full of warehouses and small, dirty buildings and sat between the land dedicated to the docking platforms and the docks. It wasn't the most desirable location in the city.

"We're here," Fiona said.

She pointed to a small, squat building between a busy warehouse and a rowdy fight house. It was dirty and looked as if it hadn't been painted in a quarter century. The shabby sign on the door read 'Wet Willy's Bar.'

Jarrett let out a snort of laughter. "Wet Willy? Seriously?"

Fiona gave him a curious look. "What is so funny?"

"Wet Willy," he laughed. "There are too many jokes to choose just one."

She stared at him blankly.

He let out a sigh as his laughter faded. "And I guess every one of them is a couple of centuries past your time. Way to make me feel old, Moon."

"Hey, don't get mad at me because you're ancient," she teased. "So, you ready to go have a drink and pretend to be a couple having a good time?"

"Yeah, I suddenly need a whiskey or two," he grumbled.

Fiona said the words to lift the no-speak spell, laughed, and slid her arm around his waist, slipping into character. "Come on, old man... I mean, sweetheart."

The inside of the bar was as shabby as the outside, yet surprisingly clean. Jarrett and Fiona ordered a couple of drinks from Carl the Bartender and found a table in a far corner that gave them a good view of both the door and the bar.

A band played in the opposite corner, filling the smoky room with twangy music reminiscent of what could have been heard in the city long before the Cataclysm. Despite the loud music, Fiona and Jarrett were careful to keep their conversation light and flirty, like that of a couple out on a date. Even in a noisy bar, vampire hearing was excellent, and using a no-speak spell would be obvious and suspicious. It was safer not to discuss the case. Fortunately, Jarrett and Fiona had worked together in similar situations before and had no problem getting into their roles, even without any preparation.

To the casual observer, they appeared to be a couple that was in lust, if not love, and completely absorbed in each other. In reality, they were both on high alert. Very little happened in the bar that they did not take note of, which is why Jarrett noticed the all too familiar man the moment he walked through the door.

Jarrett was leaning into Fiona, as if whispering something naughty in her ear, when the bar's door opened and three people walked in. Two walked to a table and sat down; the third, a tall, bald man, went to the bar.

The moment he had a clear view of the man, Jarrett's blood went ice cold.

"Python," Jarrett muttered, leaning back into his seat. His whole body on high alert. This wasn't possible. Not possible. And if it were, did that mean...?

"What?" Fiona asked, breaking into Jarrett's thoughts.

Jarrett motioned slightly with his head. "Over there. Talking to the bartender. His name is Python."

Fiona looked over in that direction. "The scary looking bald dude with all the tattoos?"

"One tattoo. It's a python. It stretches over both arms, his head, and wraps around his chest and back."

"I'm guessing that's how he got his name. Creative. You guys old friends?"

"Not exactly," Jarrett grumbled. He strained to hear what was being said, but they were too far from the bar and the music was just loud enough for their words to be muffled, even for his vampiric hearing. As Jarrett was trying to figure out how to get closer without being seen, Python finished his conversation, turned, and went out the door.

Jarrett slid out of the booth and hurried after Python, not waiting to make sure Fiona followed. He wasn't letting Python get away. The man had answers Jarrett needed.

He burst out the door into the dark night and saw his target only a few yards away. Jarrett reached him in seconds, grabbing his shoulder and pulling him around to smash a hard fist into his face. Dazed, Python crashed back against the building wall and Jarrett was on him in an instant. He shoved one arm against Python's throat. With the other hand he grabbed the dagger he wore at his waist and shoved it against Python's ribcage.

Staring into the eyes of a man who should be dead, he growled, "Where is she, Python?"

Jarrett saw the recognition in Python's eyes, but the other man pretended ignorance. "I don't know what you're talking about, mate."

"Cora. Where is she? If you made it out of that sea

alive, she did too."

This time Python let out a snort and smirked. "You'd think so since she wasn't the one with the knife in her heart. Well, perilously close to the heart. I should thank you for having such lousy aim, mate."

Jarrett pressed the tip of his dagger into Python's skin, tearing his shirt. "I won't miss this time. Now, don't make me ask again. Where's Cora?"

"Dead. I pulled her from the sea, but she'd broken her neck and drowned. So I tossed her back in."

Jarrett couldn't read the man's expression, couldn't tell from his mocking tone if he was telling the truth. But something in his gut told him Python was lying.

"I don't believe you," Jarrett growled.

Python's eyes hardened. "I don't give a furry fuck what you believe, mate."

Before Jarrett could react, he heard Fiona's voice, "What the hell is going on here? Break it up."

She grabbed his arm and pulled his dagger hand away from Python. Python took advantage of the moment and put a fist into Jarrett's midsection. He stumbled back, his knife clattering to the ground. Furious, he ran at Python, taking them both to the ground.

In the background, Jarrett could vaguely hear Fiona's voice. She was screaming something, but he couldn't make out the words. He was too intent on beating the hell out of Python. They rolled on the ground, exchanging punches until Jarrett felt a warm burst of energy that had him flying backward and landing on his back several feet away from Python. He looked over at Fiona and knew she'd used magic on them.

He stumbled to his feet, as Python did the same. Python pulled a dagger from his boot as he rose and threw it, but he was staggering and his aim was off. Instead of hitting Jarrett, the knife veered well to the left and grazed Fiona's arm, leaving a long, thin slice in its wake.

"Son of a bitch," Fiona screamed, shaking her arm. Then she raised both hands and sent out bursts of energy that sent both men flying into the building.

She pulled a six-inch-long, thin oak stick from inside her vest. Jarrett knew she carried it to help focus her power when she couldn't carry her hanbo. She pointed the stick at them, alternating between them. "That is enough! You are both pending arrest under my authority as an agent of the Black Blade Guard. If either of you moves, the blast I just gave you will feel like a tickle compared to the next one."

"You can't arrest me," Jarrett said, struggling to stand. Some of his fury had been knocked out of him, and he was starting to realize what a colossal mistake he'd just made.

"You wanna watch me?" She asked, narrowing her eyes at him and pointing the stick at him threateningly until he slid back down into a sitting position.

He'd never seen her quite so angry, at least not directed at him. Though he really didn't believe she had the authority to arrest him—he did outrank her—he felt it was probably best not to test the theory right now.

She gave him one last look, daring him to move, and then walked over to Python.

"Mr... Python, was it?"

Python grunted. "Yeah, that's my name, what's it to ya, Blade?"

Fiona grabbed the front of his shirt and pulled him up, slamming him against the building much like Jarrett had done moments before. She poked the stick under his chin. "Manners. I'm being polite to you, you be polite to me, got it?"

"Yeah, sure. My name is Python, ma'am," he sneered the last word.

Fiona smirked. "A little better." She patted him down, throwing away a dagger from his waist and one in his boot. "Now, can you tell me what happened?"

Python's expression took on a false innocence. "I was minding my own business when he attacked me. I had to protect myself."

Jarrett sputtered, but Fiona sent him a quelling

look and he quieted again.

"Okay, he just attacked you out of the blue, and you have no idea why?" she asked Python.

"No. He started asking about some dame, and then he hit me."

"And what were you doing in Wet Willy's bar?"

"I'm new to the city. I was asking directions."

Fiona let out a long sigh, and then took a step back. "Okay, you can go."

Pulling himself to his feet, Jarrett stared at her open-mouthed as Python retrieved his discarded weapons, shot Jarrett a grin, and disappeared down the street.

The moment she walked back to him and said the spell to shield their conversation, he snapped, "How could you let him go?"

"I had no choice."

"Yes you did. He assaulted a Black Blade Guard Agent."

"Really? Are we talking about the one that is off duty and attacked him unprovoked? Or the one that was inadvertently caught in the crossfire as he defended himself from said attack?" She shot back at him, annoyed.

"He was lying."

Fiona rolled her eyes. "Of-fucking-course he was lying, Jarrett. Do I look like an idiot? It doesn't matter. You blew it. Even if he were the supplier we were looking for and I had definitive proof, I'd still have to let him go. This was an observe-and-track mission. We have nothing to arrest on, even if we found him with an unknown substance, which we didn't."

"Fiona..." Jarrett said.

"Shut it," she snapped. "I don't want to hear it. If he was the drug supplier, you blew any chance we had at catching him. He'll know we are on to him. And if he wasn't, because of you, my cover is blown. I have no chance of tracking down the guy now. I'll have to turn the case over to another agent to do the undercover work."

Jarrett understood how angry she was. He would be the same if someone had screwed up one of his cases. "I'm sorry."

She glared at him. "I said I don't want to hear it. We'll deal with this elsewhere. I need to go talk to Carl. Stay here and cool down," she said. She broke the silence spell, turned on her heel, and headed back inside.

Jarrett rubbed his hands over his face. What had he been thinking? No, he knew what he'd been thinking. Or rather, not thinking. He'd let his rage and anger rule him. Something he hadn't done in ages. It would have been smarter to trail Python and see where he went. Whether he was the drug dealer or not, he might have lead Jarrett to proof of whether or not Cora was alive. Fiona was right, he'd been stupid.

Fiona returned a few minutes later, her face contorted in anger.

"Your buddy, Python, was not the drug supplier. He asked Carl the location of the nearest brothel. Don't even open your mouth. Back to Pinky's. Now." She stalked off without another word.

They walked back to the pub at a fast clip, not speaking. When they arrived, Jarrett followed Fiona up to the rooftop garden.

The moment they were alone, Fiona rounded on him. "I never took you to be a moron, Campbell. I can't even imagine what would be so important to make you blow an undercover op like that."

"What's going on? What's all the shouting about?" Anya asked as she ran onto the roof.

"Your boyfriend is a flipping idiot," Fiona yelled.

"He's not…"

"I'm not…"

Jarrett and Anya sputtered at the same time, but Fiona held up her hand impatiently.

"Not the issue right now," she fumed. "Wait, why are you up here?"

Anya narrowed her eyes at her sister. "Because you two came running through the pub like a bat out of hell and there is blood on your arm. I thought you might need help." Her voice level rivaled her sister's.

Fiona glanced down at her arm, and then back at

Anya, her face and voice softer. "Sorry, An. It's just a small cut. I'm a little pissed at Jarrett right now, and I just need to yell at him for a bit. I came up here so we wouldn't wake River."

"If you don't take it down a notch you're going to wake up the whole damned city," Anya retorted and tossed Fiona the towel in her hand. "Here, you can clean up your arm with that. What are you yelling at him about? Is it personal or work related? Do I need to stay and take sides?"

Jarrett nearly laughed out loud. Anya was actually contemplating taking sides in an argument between him and Fiona. He wondered if she would take his side against her sister. Of course he knew he was in the wrong this time, but would she back him up if she thought he was right?

"It's work related," Fiona said.

"Okay," Anya said, looking prepared to leave them alone.

"I totally screwed up. I deserve whatever she dishes out," Jarrett said before he realized what he was doing.

Anya and Fiona just stared at him a long minute, then Anya walked over and pulled him down into a kiss. It was a quick, sweet kiss, but it made him burn to his toes.

"I like it when a man admits he's wrong," she said. Then she turned back to Fiona. "Okay, you can kick his ass now, but try not to break him. I have plans later."

"Wow, you just turned fucking up into a ploy to get into my sister's pants. That takes skill, my friend," Fiona said when the roof door swung shut behind Anya.

Jarrett walked over to a bench under a small grove of potted trees. "Yeah, not sure how that happened. I meant it though. I fucked up and deserve whatever you want to say. Go ahead, rage at me."

Fiona sat down next to him.

"Damn it, I can't. Not when you are being all adult and taking responsibility and shit." She slapped him on the arm. "You took all the fun out of it. Asshole."

They sat in silence for a while, and then she said, "So, tell me what is up with you and this Python dude. What kind of history could make you forget several centuries of training?"

"The last time I saw him, I killed him."

Fiona let out a long, low whistle. "Well, yeah, okay. I can see where that would kind of throw you off. So, who's this Cora you were screaming at him about?"

"I can't tell you. It's classified," he said.

"Yeah, yeah. Special ops need to know mumbo jumbo. Whatever." She pulled her porta-scry from her vest pocket. "You reckon Sam has clearance? Because when I tell him you wrecked my op, he'll find out why. Then he'll tell me."

"Sam already knows," Jarrett sighed.

She grinned and flipped open the leather case covering the scry-crystal. "Oh, good. That means he can tell me now."

Jarrett groaned. If it were any other agent, he'd tell them to give it their best shot. But Sam would tell Fiona. And not just because he doted on her like a childless uncle with his favorite niece. But because Fiona was one of the best agents Nash City had to offer. The fact that she wasn't a member of any special division was owed solely to the fact that she had family and didn't want to be unable to communicate with them for months, even years, at a time. She was also trustworthy. Sam trusted her with his life, as did Jarrett.

If she made the call, Sam would tell her everything. And as a consequence of Jarrett not telling her himself, she'd stay pissed at him for a few days. He might as well avoid that.

"Put the scry-crystal down. I'll tell you." He let out another put-upon sigh. "I don't have to explain that this is top-secret Kukri op intel?"

"Yeah, yeah, pain of death, cross my heart, poke my eye out with a stick. Whatever," she rolled her eyes at him as she slid the crystal back into its case and then into her pocket.

Jarrett couldn't help but laugh at her utter lack of respect for the rules.

"Have you ever heard of Dread, or Captain Dread?"

he asked.

Fiona looked thoughtful. "Yeah, I think so. Hardcore slaver and vampire elitist. He was on the most wanted list for a while."

"That's the one. As a slaver he was bad enough, but as long as he stayed out of Allied City-States, we didn't have much of a beef with him. But like you said, he was a vampire elitist. He believed all other races—norm, mage, and shifter—should be killed or subjugated under vampire rule. He started collecting quite the cult following. Touted himself as a captain in the war against inferior beings."

Fiona shuddered. "Ugh. Real peach of a guy."

Jarrett nodded. "Yep, a prince among men. Anyway, as he grew his cult, he got more and more bold. His crew started venturing into Allied City-States and their territories to abduct people to sell as slaves."

"He must have worked primarily in the south. As far as I know he never came to Nash."

"He didn't. He operated mostly in the southwest, but he was quickly venturing out. He went from being a nuisance to being a real problem. It became clear he had to be eliminated, but his following had grown to the point that he had cells in multiple areas. We needed intel."

Fiona nodded, knowingly. "An agent was sent in undercover. This Cora you were screaming at him about."

"Yes. She was a Kukri. Her mission was to infiltrate, get as close to Dread as possible, and get intel. Then, once we had an idea of his operation, she was to take him out."

"But she didn't?"

Jarrett shook his head. "No. She was in his inner circle within six months. She was a fount of information. She gave her handler a lot of intel, but about a year after she got into the inner circle, the information stopped coming. She stopped contacting her handler. I was sent to track them down, assassinate Dread, and if she were still alive, pull Cora out."

"You didn't find her?"

Jarrett let out a humorless laugh. "I found her in Detroit. In bed next to Dread."

Fiona's eyes went wide. "Wow. What did you do?"

"My job. Slit his throat and put a knife in his heart and twisted. Cora woke and I tried to get her out, but she went crazy. She was hysterical. She was screaming at me that she loved him. Python, Dread's right hand man, came in. We fought. They escaped to the roof of the building."

In Jarrett's mind he could see the rain slicked, crumbling rooftop and Cora standing there naked with Dread's blood all over her.

"What happened, how did they get away?" Fiona

asked, pulling Jarrett back to the here and now.

"They had a hot air balloon. It was raining, so they were having a hard time taking off. Python was in the balloon and Cora was still on the roof ledge. I put a throwing star through the balloon and a knife through Python's heart. Well, obviously, I put it near his heart. He fell out of the balloon and into the sea below. Cora kept shrieking at me that I'd taken everything from her. I tried to persuade her to come with me, but she said she could never go back to being a Blade. Then, she jumped off the ledge and into the sea. There were a lot of rocks."

Fiona sat for a long time, obviously speechless. "I have no idea what to say. That had to be awful. Do you think she was really in love with Dread?"

"I kept telling myself she was brainwashed, but I'm not so sure. Anyway, that was eight months ago. I was convinced she hadn't died. It is damned hard to kill a vampire, after all. But there was no trace of her body, and I couldn't find any trace of her in the area. I've been searching since. But every lead was a dead end, and I just closed the case when I came back to Nash a few days ago."

"I'm guessing you didn't put everything in the report."

Jarrett shook his head. "The report says killed in the line of duty. Without further information, that is exactly what happened. Officially she fell from the building into the sea below during a struggle with her captors while I was rescuing her."

"I'm sorry. That blows. I can see why you freaked out at Wet Willy's tonight. I'm still pissed over it, but I can understand."

Jarrett gave her a weak smile. "I really am sorry about that. I just lost my head."

She looked at him for a long moment. "I think there's more to this than you are telling me."

"Nothing relevant," he said. He'd had enough emotional revelations for the night, he wasn't about to explain his history with Cora right now.

She nodded. "Okay. Well, it's all done now. Come on, brother, let's go get drunk. I'm buying."

He followed her to the roof door. "You are part owner of the bar, you get alcohol for free."

She grinned. "I know. That's why I'm buying."

Thirteen
Anya

THE PUBLIC MARKET WAS DEAD COMPARED TO market week. The rest of the month traveling merchants filtered in and set up shop for a few days alongside the local merchants, blacksmiths, jewelers, and other trade and craft people that had permanent stalls at the market. So, though it wasn't as bustling as it had been two weeks ago, there was still plenty for Farrah and me to browse on our afternoon out.

It was my regular night off, and I'd talked Pinky into giving Farrah a few hours off for the afternoon so we could have a girls' day out.

"What do you think of this one?" I held up a dark grey corset.

Farrah looked up from where she was browsing the clothing booth's wares. "Oh, definitely. It will go perfectly over that strapless, red dress you bought earlier. Pair it with those black short boots you own, and you have the perfect night-out-on-the-town outfit."

"I think you're right." I turned to the proprietor of the stall. "I'll take it."

"Jarrett's tongue will flop out when he sees you in that outfit," Farrah said as we moved to the next stall.

I laughed. "That's the plan. You know, since you're going to be working in the pub a night or two a week, you should buy yourself a few pretty things."

Farrah snorted. "It doesn't seem to matter what I wear, after a few drinks the men are going to make passes at me no matter what."

I looked at her for a long moment as she browsed through a pile of colorful scarves. From what Fiona had told me, Farrah had once been quite the party girl. As one would expect, being abducted by a madman had changed her. An air of depression seemed to hover around her, though she always smiled when spoken to, and always seemed to try to be helpful and cheerful. I suspected that part of the problem was that she'd lived with a certain amount of confidence in her appearance, but either no longer had it, or no longer wanted men to see her as attractive.

"You know what," I said, picking up a floral scarf. "I

don't wear my clothes, or put on makeup, or do my hair for men. I do all of it for myself. Because it makes me feel good. Yes, that red dress will make Jarrett forget his name tonight, but it's not the fabric that will do the job. It will be the way I wear it. The way I feel in my skin while in the dress, and the confidence and sexiness I'll project."

"I don't think I can be as confident as you. I don't think I ever was." She looked at me doubtfully. "I used to act like I was queen bee, but I never really felt it. And I don't want to be that girl ever again."

I tried another way of explaining.

"I'm not saying you should be, Farrah. I'm not talking about projecting a false confidence, or trying to get the attention of others. It only matters how you feel about yourself. Have you ever noticed that Fiona is, more often than not, in dirty khakis and the same, worn-out leather vest?"

Farrah's brow furrowed. "Not really. I don't really notice her clothes."

"But you are a girl who usually notices clothes, right?"

She nodded. "Yeah, I guess so. I have always liked wearing pretty things, I suppose. Yeah, I like clothes."

"But you don't notice that Fiona barely takes time to brush her hair most days, because she projects confidence. She is most comfortable in khaki or leather pants, combat boots, and her multi-pocketed vests. The only thing that ever changes is the color of her shirt. And don't get me started on that belt she wears." I shook my head. "The point is, she feels so confident in her own skin, when she's in those clothes her confidence is all you notice. What about River?"

Farrah smiled. Everyone usually did when they thought of my baby sister. "She always looks very pretty."

"Yes, she does. But did you realize that she only has about five of those flowy dresses she wears over and over? She'll wait until one has unmendable holes before making a new one. Not because she has to, but because that is what she is comfortable in. She also doesn't use any of the cosmetics she makes for me, except the hydrating cream."

Farrah's expression told me what I was saying was starting to register. "So, what you are saying is I need to wear things that make me feel confident and like 'me'. But, I'm not sure what that is."

"You strike me as a girl who really likes pretty things. But you brought very little with you when you came to live with us. You only have a couple of pants and tops, and they are all a little drab. You don't seem comfortable in them. You are, of course, welcome to borrow anything I have, but I think you would feel better if you had a few pieces that you really liked, that you picked out. Clothes won't solve all your problems, whatever they may be, but feeling good about yourself is a huge step in the right direction."

The shopkeeper, who had been standing behind the table listening to our conversation, said, "She's not wrong, honey. Wearing something that makes you feel nice, no matter how pretty or ugly anyone else thinks it is, can really lift your spirit."

"I'll prove it. Pick a scarf, any scarf," I told Farrah, gesturing to some of the more expensive scarves hung along the back of the stall. "Pick out the scarf you think is the prettiest."

After dithering a moment, Farrah pointed to a large green and gold scarf hanging just behind the shopkeeper.

The shopkeeper smiled, wiped her hands on her apron, and retrieved the scarf. "A lovely choice."

"Here, let's try it on." I helped Farrah drape the scarf across her shoulders.

It looked beautiful on her. The gold in the scarf matched some of the golden highlights in her blonde hair, and the shades of emerald and gold picked up the same hues in the flecks of her eyes. But my point was proven when the shopkeeper held up a dusty mirror. The moment Farrah saw her reflection, her entire face changed. She smiled the biggest, most genuine smile I'd seen since I met her.

"You look just lovely, my dear," the shopkeeper said.

"Thank you."

"Do you like it?" I asked.

She looked at me, her smile wide. "I do. I think you were right. I do need to have more pretty things in my life."

"Good to see someone listens to me," I said. Then I looked at the shopkeeper. "We'll take it. My treat."

"Oh, no, that's okay. I have money," Farrah said.

"Yes, you do. But I know how much Pinky pays you, and you'd blow half a week's pay on that scarf. As for me, I won an obscene amount of money on a fight I was in last week. Pinky won't let me spend fight winnings on household things, and I already have way too many clothes. So, you are going to let me treat you today, and not just the scarf."

"Um, okay, I guess," Farrah stammered, a little unsure of herself.

She was trying to be independent, I understood that. But I also knew that no one had been nice to her, really nice to her with no expectations of return, in a long time. If ever.

"That wasn't me asking for your permission, Farrah. That was me giving you a statement of fact," I told her with a wink.

She smiled and her whole face lit up. "Okay."

I paid for the scarf and we moved on to another stall. Watching Farrah rifle through clothes and helping her pick out outfits was more fun than I could have imagined. Within an hour and a half, we had three canvas shopping bags full of clothes and shoes.

"Ugh," I said, leaning against a table in an empty merchant's booth. "It's almost noon, and I'm starving. Let's grab some food, go to River's booth, and eat lunch with her."

Farrah looked as tired as I felt. "Sounds like a plan."

We grabbed corn fritters and lemonade at a vendor near River's stall and took it over to her. She was sitting on a bench looking bored. "Ah! Food! I may have to name my firstborn after both of you. You know, if I ever have kids. Which really, I probably won't."

"You're rambling, Rivs," I said, handing her a paper-wrapped fritter.

"I know, sorry. It's just been kind of slow today so I've had no one to talk to, and I was getting hungry, but I didn't want to leave the stand unmanned because there were a couple of kids earlier that stole some apples."

"So you wanted to stay and protect the stand?" Farrah asked.

I laughed. "No, she stayed so that if they came back she could give them each a full basket of food."

The pale skin of River's cheeks turned bright pink. "What can I say, I'm a softy."

"You should have called a guard when they swiped

the apples," I told her, knowing it was a futile statement.

"They were probably starving."

"Or they were little hoodlums in the making."

"Doesn't matter. I have an open door policy, and you know it. If they need or want food from my stall, they get it. No questions asked." Her tone brooked no more arguments.

That was something I loved about River. She had a soft heart, but if you tried to step on her right to be soft-hearted, she'd show you just how tough she was. And really, her policy had never steered her wrong. Her vegetable and herb stall brought in almost as much money as the pub. She gave away a lot of food, but more often than not, people who she gave food to either brought her money later when they had it, or brought her other goods or trinkets that they had made in trade.

"Sorry, Rivs," I said.

"It's okay. So, looks like you two have had a lot of fun," she said, motioning to our over full bags.

"Yeah, I let Anya buy me way too much stuff," Farrah said, her cheeks now turning the same color River's had.

"As if you had any choice," I said, laughing. "Besides, you have no idea how much fun it is to shop with someone who actually likes clothes after growing up with my two sisters."

River laughed. "Hey, I'm paying for everything on your next shopping spree if it'll keep her from dragging me along."

Farrah laughed.

We ate, chatted, and laughed for almost an hour, only pausing for the occasional customer. It was the first time the three of us had spent any quality time together. It wasn't the same as having Fiona there, but I was really starting to like Farrah. And I could see her coming out of her shell a little.

"I hate to break up the fun, but I need to get back. I have a hot date tonight," I said. Jarrett and I were going to have dinner, go dancing, and then spend a long night together on his boat. It was my last night off before his leave was up in two days, and I was determined to spend as much time with him as possible, and most of that naked.

"Wow, I've never seen you get a dreamy look on your face like that before, An," River said. "Anything we should know about you and Jarrett?"

I rolled my eyes at her. "Nothing that wouldn't make you blush for a week," I said, laughing. "I'm just looking forward to a night out on the town and having someone pour me drinks for a change."

She smiled sweetly. "Good. You deserve it. Oh, before you go, can you swing by Sarah Jane's and give her this." She produced a basket of fruits, vegetables, bread, pouches of herbs, and what looked like a bowl of soup. "She's out sick, that's why I had to work here today."

"Sure, I know where she lives. It won't be a problem."

"Thank you," River said, hugging Farrah and me in turn. "I'll see you later."

Farrah and I crossed the bridge, and I led her down a back alley into the slums. River's shop assistant, Sarah Jane, was an orphan norm girl of about sixteen. She had come to work for River just a couple of months ago after her mother died. Her mother had been a seamstress with her own very popular stall at the market. She'd left a little bit of money for Sarah Jane and despite its location in the slums, their small house was sturdy.

I had Farrah wait outside while I went inside, in case Sarah Jane was contagious. She was very obviously ill, but didn't seem to have a fever. Knowing she didn't have anyone to watch out for her, I gave her my scry-crystal so she could call River for help if she needed it. Norms usually didn't carry porta-scrys because they couldn't always use them. Fiona had mine charged with extra strong spells by the Blade Chargers so that I could activate it anytime. Sarah Jane protested, but I told her she could give it back to me when she was well.

After leaving Sarah Jane's, Farrah and I headed

back to Pinky's where I was going to meet Jarrett in just a few hours. We were absorbed in conversation, talking about the purchases we'd made, and I didn't notice the two men walking behind us until two others stepped out from behind a building, blocking our path. Wordlessly, Farrah and I turned in time to see the two men only a few feet behind us. We were in a narrow path between two buildings. There were no windows and no doors. The only way out was through the men.

"Excuse me," I said, knowing it was futile, but trying anyway.

One of the men laughed, the sound chilling my blood.

"Come with us nice and easy, honey, and we'll leave the blonde lass unharmed," said a man with thick arms and dark hair.

"How about you let us pass and I'll leave you unharmed," I countered. To Farrah, I whispered, "You fight with everything you got."

She looked me in the eye, her gaze hard, and she gave a nod. I knew she wouldn't crumple into a hysterical mess. We may have little chance of getting out of this predicament, but she wouldn't go down without a fight. Neither would I.

"Get them," the dark haired man ordered the other three.

Farrah and I stood back-to-back, and as the men

closed in, Farrah's hand went up. A loose brick that had been lying on the side of the road began to hover in the air. The four men stopped moving, watching the brick. Using the distraction, I plunged forward kicking the man nearest to me in the stomach.

The next few minutes, or perhaps only seconds, passed in a blur. I was fighting off two of them but every time I knocked one down, the other was there, getting a blow in. Every now and then, I would catch a glimpse of Farrah. She was levitating anything she could get her hands on to throw at them, which was mostly dirt and rocks. It was keeping them at bay. She was also screaming her head off, trying to catch the attention of someone passing by, but no one came.

I finally had both men on the ground at the same time and was turning to help Farrah when I realized she wasn't screaming. I whirled to see her lying on the ground, one of the men standing over her. Her eyes were open, and I could see her eyelids blinking, but she wasn't moving.

"What did you do to h..." A sharp pain in my leg cut off my words. I looked down to see a long, thin dart sticking out of my thigh. "What the...?" Darkness surrounded me.

Fourteen
Jarrett

JARRETT STOOD BACK AND ADMIRED HIS HANDY WORK. The fresh paint gleamed in the mid-afternoon sun. He let out a sigh that expressed both his satisfaction and his disappointment. The wheel house looked nice, but it was the last of the maintenance he had planned for The Minnow before his leave was up. Finishing it brought to mind that he only had two days left.

The irony of the 'only' in that thought wasn't lost on him. He'd been a Black Blade Guard for almost five centuries, and a Kukri for all but about fifty of those years. Up until this point, he'd had to be forced to take his mandatory two-week leave every six months. And he always took any opportunity possible to go back to work early.

This was the first time in his long career he was dreading going back to work. It was the first time in his even longer life that he was dreading leaving a woman behind. Two weeks was such a short time to him. Barely a grain of sand in the vampiric hour glass, yet so much had happened in that tiny grain. A whole life time had happened.

He'd done the most stupid thing he could have possibly done. He'd gone and fallen in love with a norm woman. He felt his lips curve into a smile, just thinking of Anya. As stupid as it had been to get close to her, as much as he knew he would ache for her when he left, he couldn't regret it. He might have the pain of losing her for decades, perhaps even forever, but he'd have the joy of loving her and the memory of her beautiful face to last him.

He laughed out loud at the sappy, romantic thread of his thoughts. What he'd always suspected was true. Love turned you into a weeny.

Amused at himself, he began cleaning up. He only had a few days left with Anya and he was going to make them memorable. Starting with dinner and dancing, and then a long night of creative lovemaking. He was determined to take as many good memories with him as possible, and leave enough that she didn't forget about him for a while.

He was cleaning his paint brushes in a bucket of river water when he thought he heard his name. Dropping the brushes into the water, he concentrated, listening closely. Yes, someone was yelling his name. He turned and searched the dock, but it was packed with people. He couldn't tell where the sound had come from.

Then he heard it again and looked in time to see a young woman stumble awkwardly through a group of dockworkers. She wasn't running, but she did seem to be moving as quickly as she could. Her gait was choppy and stumbling, and she swayed from side to side as if she were drunk. She wore dirty, torn pants and her dark blonde hair was hiding her face, but there was something familiar about her.

"Farrah?" he called out.

The girl raised her head in his direction. Her face was red and streaked with dirt and tears, but it was definitely Farrah. Her eyes went wide when she saw him. Trying to move faster, she stumbled and fell forward on her hands and knees.

Jarrett jumped to the pier and ran to her. He knelt beside her. "Farrah, are you okay? What happened?"

"Anya," she said, her voice so thick with tears and hysteria he could barely understand her, but there was no mistaking that name.

His blood ran cold. "What about Anya? What happened? Where is she?"

Farrah sobbed. "They took her. They told me to give you this and said they would call after sunset."

She pressed a porta-scry into his hand, and then fell forward onto the pier as if all the energy had left her body. The only way Jarrett could tell she was conscious was that she was still crying softly.

Fury and fear raged inside him. Someone had taken Anya, and they'd done it to get to him. It had to be Python. Forcing himself to stay calm, he clicked into professional mode.

Putting the scry-crystal into his pocket, he pulled his own porta-scry out of the opposite pocket. He flipped it open and pushed energy through.

When Sam's face popped up, he didn't bother with preliminaries. "I'll be in your office in ten minutes. I need a med-mage and Fiona there. Oh, and you better call Pinky."

"What's going on?" Sam asked.

"I'm not really sure, but it looks like Anya has been kidnapped. Farrah just showed up at my boat in hysterics. Just get everyone there, please."

"Got it," Sam said, and the connection was severed.

Jarrett flipped the leather case over the crystal and slipped the scry back in his pocket. Leaning over, he put his hand on the crying girl's shoulder.

"Farrah, sweetie," he said, his voice soft. "I'm going to pick you up now. Is that okay?"

"Yes," she said, her voice weak and hoarse.

Gently, he scooped her up into his arms. He wanted to run like he had the night before when Anya had been hurt and in his arms, but he didn't dare. He'd known essentially how Anya was hurt, and had been careful not to jar her leg. He had no idea what might have been done to Farrah and didn't want to risk further injury. He began walking as briskly as he could.

"Jarrett," Farrah said, hiccupping. "I'm not hurt. I don't think I am. They drugged me. I'm crying because I'm mad. They took her and I couldn't stop them, and I'm really angry."

Jarrett looked down at the red, tear-stained face and nearly laughed out loud. He could see the truth of her words reflected in her eyes. She had definitely fallen in with the right family. He didn't know if she'd been like this before she'd been abducted by Bokor, but after six months living with Pinky and the Moon sisters, she couldn't be more like them if she'd grown up there.

"Okay, then. In that case, I'm going to run. Can you hang on tight?"

"I'm a little weak, but I'll do my best."

He gathered her a little tighter to him and took off. Weaving in and out of the late afternoon crowds, they made it to the headquarters building in just a few minutes. It wasn't until he was standing in front of the lift he realized he was still in the cutoff shorts and old shirt he'd been painting in. He'd left his ID crystal, along with his weapons and long pants, back on The Minnow.

"Can you stand?" he asked Farrah.

She nodded. "I think so."

He set her on her feet in the lift, close to the wall so she could lean on it, and pulled his scry out.

"Sam," he said when the other man answered. "I'm in the lift, can you give me an override?"

"Be right there."

Less than a minute after the crystal went dark, the lift began to move upwards. Sam and a healer—Jarrett was glad to see it wasn't the one who had treated Anya—met them when the lift doors opened.

"I've got her," Jarrett said, and carried Farrah into Sam's office.

The healer was examining her when Fiona and Pinky arrived. Pinky immediately rushed to her side. "Are you okay? What happened?"

He didn't ask about Anya, and Jarrett assumed Sam hadn't told them Anya was missing. Before Farrah could answer, Jarrett asked the med-mage, "Is she okay to answer a few questions?"

"Yes," the healer said, "But I want to get her across the street to the hospital soon. It will take a while to completely remove the drug from her system, and she will need rest."

"Thank you, Healer Ramsey," Sam said. "Please wait outside for a few minutes, and then we'll let you take your patient."

The healer nodded and left, shutting the door behind him.

The four of them sat, listening intently, as Farrah told them the story of how four men had ambushed them in the slums.

"We were winning," she said, a small note of pride evident in her voice. "Anya was really fighting, and I was using my power to throw rocks and dust in their faces. It wasn't much, but it was working until one of them threw a dart at me. It was the weirdest feeling. I couldn't feel anything, it was as if my entire body had disappeared. I fell to the ground."

"Where was Anya at that moment, Farrah? Do you remember?" Fiona asked.

"Yeah. She had just knocked down both of her guys and was coming towards me, and then she just fell to the ground. That's when one of them laid the scry on my stomach and told me I'd get feeling back in my body in half an hour." She turned and looked at Jarrett. "He said I was to go directly to you, and they would be watching to know if I went to the guards instead. He told me to tell you that someone would contact you on that porta-scry after sundown."

"Did you see which way they went with Anya?" Sam asked.

She shook her head. "No. I was lying on my back and couldn't move. I know they picked her up, and one of them said to be careful with her or the boss wouldn't be happy."

"That bodes well," Sam said.

Fiona walked over and put her hand on Farrah's shoulder. "You did a good job, sweetie. Come on, I'll take you out to wait with the healer for a moment, okay?"

Farrah nodded and let Fiona pull her out of the chair and help her walk out to the hall.

"What do we do first?" Pinky asked when Fiona was back in the office.

"You take Farrah to the hospital and wait with her," Fiona said. "This is her second trauma in six months, she could really use a friendly face."

Pinky glared. "No. Not till my little girl is back home."

Fiona returned his glare, not budging an inch. "Please, I'm as worried as you are right now, so I don't want to fight with you. We can't do much except theorize until Jarrett receives the call. After that, it will all be about strategy. You aren't trained for this. I promise I'll keep you updated, but the most helpful thing you can do right now is help keep Farrah and River calm."

"River," Pinky said, as if just realizing she wasn't there. "Where is she?"

"She's on her way. I scryed the guard post at the market after Jarrett called. A city guard officer is escorting her here. I'll have her taken to the hospital to meet you," Sam said.

"Please, Dad?" Fiona pleaded.

Jarrett swallowed a thick lump that had formed in his throat. She never called Pinky 'Dad'. It was a sign of how worried she was.

Pinky sighed and pulled Fiona into a tight hug. "Okay. Just keep me updated, please."

As he was walking to the door to join Farrah, Jarrett stopped him by saying, "I'm really sorry, Pinky."

Pinky turned to him. "For?"

"Anya was targeted because she is close to me. It's my fault."

"It looks like whoever took her did it to get to you. True. But every person in this room is close to Anya, and every one of us has people who would like to hurt us in any way possible. I'm sure Anya has a few of those herself. It's a dangerous world, and my girls are tough and know how to take care of themselves." He moved so that he was toe-to-toe with Jarrett, and the difference in their sizes was painfully evident. Though not short by any stretch of the imagination, Pinky was about four inches shorter than Jarrett and at least seventy-five pounds lighter. Yet there was something in his eyes that told Jarrett he did not want to get on the man's bad side. "You have nothing to be sorry for, yet. If you don't bring my girl home to me safe and sound, then you can be sorry. I'll make sure you are." Then he turned and walked out.

The next three hours felt like an eternity. Jarrett thought he might go crazy before the call came in.

He had spent hours going over every possible suspect with Sam and Fiona. They kept landing back on Python.

"You tried to kill him, isn't that motive enough?" Fiona said, for probably the fifth time.

"Yes, that is very true. But I'm telling you, Python is a born lackey, hired muscle. He looks big and bad, but when it comes to brains to cook up schemes and plans, he doesn't have them. Nor does he have the motivation. He doesn't do anything unless he's paid, or ordered to. But he's never been loyal enough to anyone to take orders, except Dread."

Sam leaned back in his chair. "I don't want to believe it's true, but I'm inclined to agree with you, brother. Cora must be pulling his strings. If he survived, she could have as well. And she always had a vindictive streak."

Before Jarrett could respond, the scry-crystal Farrah had given him buzzed in his pocket. He pulled it out and activated it.

His heart lurched when the image of Anya tied to a chair with a gag in her mouth came on screen. She was glaring at the person holding the scry and wiggling so that her chair hopped.

"You picked a little ball of fire this time, Jarrett."

The familiar voice nearly stopped Jarrett's heart.

"Cora."

The scry turned, revealing a glimpse of an empty warehouse, before settling on Cora's face. "Surprised to see me?"

"No," Jarrett half lied. "I knew you were alive."

"No thanks to you. Ahh, but that is a discussion for another time. I guess you want your girlfriend back. You know, I never pegged you for sticking to a type, but really Jarrett, a redheaded barmaid? Were you feeling nostalgic?"

Jarrett ignored the bait. "Cora, I'll trade myself for Anya. When and where?"

Cora's face screwed up into a childlike pout. "Straight to business, huh? No reminiscing over the good old times? Fine. Meet me at the airfield in an hour. I won't waste my breath telling you to come alone, but I will tell you that if I see anyone but you, I'll kill the girl. So you make sure Sam's agents are like shadows."

There was a muffled voice off to the side, then Cora said, "Oh, yes, the little dark-haired Blade you were at the bar with last week. She's this one's sister?" She jerked her head towards Anya.

Fiona grabbed the crystal out of Jarrett's grasp and looked into it. "Damn right I am."

"You can come, too, honey." Cora said, giving a nasty smile before the scry-crystal went dark.

The three stood in silence for a long moment before Sam said, "Gear up, you two. Meet me in the prep room in fifteen."

Jarrett looked down at his cutoffs. "I have some clothes in my room, but I'll need some weapons."

"Not a problem," Sam said.

Jarrett went to his room and changed into his regular uniform of heavy, black denim pants, black shirt, and black leather vest. When he walked into the op-prep room fifteen minutes later, there were ten agents besides Sam and Fiona. Eight were equipped with either a crossbow or compound bow, and the other two carried med packs. They were arranged around a table with a large, hand-drawn map in the center.

"We don't know which platform she will be at, if she will even be on a platform. It's too risky for you to be inside the airfield. I want you spread around the perimeter here." He pointed to the map to indicate where. "Medics, I want you here and here. No one fires unless I give the order."

"Not even if we have a clear shot?" One of the agents asked.

"No," Jarrett answered, his voice hard. "The suspect and the victim have similar hair colors. It's too risky."

Sam cleared his throat. "Okay, people. Make sure you have plenty of bolts and arrows and let's move out."

Jarrett and Fiona hung back until the other agents had left the room.

"I have a feeling you have more of a history with this Cora chick than you told me the other night. I don't know what it is, and I don't care," Fiona said, giving Jarrett an assessing stare. "If I get a chance, I'll kill her."

Jarrett returned her gaze unwaveringly. "Unless I do it first."

Fifteen
Jarrett

***D**ESPITE THE FEAR AND ANXIETY THAT ROLLED THROUGH him, Jarrett was struck with the same sense of awe and irony that he had every time he was at an airfield or saw an airship. When he was a child, a hot air balloon was a novelty. Something most people never even glimpsed. And over the span of his long life, he'd seen so much come and go. He remembered the one shining century of astronomical technological advancements, one after another. He'd lived through the era of the Wright brothers' first flight, Amelia Earhart, zeppelins, jets, and space shuttles. In a time where people flew around the world in huge metal machines, air balloons were once again, or perhaps still, a novelty used only for amusement and recreation. Then the cataclysm came along and washed away all the technology. So much knowledge had been lost.

Now, it was a time for hot air balloons again, but while some in the world might not ever see one, and many would never ride in one, they were not used for recreation anymore. They were the only mode of air travel. The smaller hot air balloons were usually owned by a rich family, or by a company to transport a few individuals at a time from a large city like Nash City to a smaller community, sometimes as far as Atlanta. The larger airships were basically a wooden cabin that held fifteen to twenty passengers attached to three or four hot air balloons, each with a copilot that answered to the ship's navigator, usually a mage with power to navigate wind currents.

The full circle society had taken never ceased to amaze him. But now wasn't the time to think about that.

The three agents walking behind him split away to take up positions around the airfield. He forced himself to concentrate as he stalked towards his destination. Fiona kept stride next to him, Sam on the other side of her. She stopped, tapped his arm, and pointed. There were six two-story-high platforms with balloons docked at four of them, and two three-story airship platforms, both of which were empty. Each balloon glowed against the dark sky, the fire used to heat the air illuminating them. By that glow, he could see three figures, one in a balloon and two on the platform next to it.

Sam motioned that he was going to circle around. Jarrett and Fiona nodded, and he slipped off into the darkness while they continued forward towards the docking platform.

Jarrett's entire body was on high alert, and the same tension rolled off Fiona in waves. He rarely worked with a partner these days, but when he did, he liked for it to be her. They worked well together, and trusted each other implicitly. Although they had been in situations much like this before, it had never felt this dire.

Even last year, when Fiona had been kidnapped and Jarrett had helped Ian rescue her, he hadn't felt anywhere near as scared as he did now. As much as he loved Fiona like a sister, it was nothing to how he felt for Anya.

He also couldn't deny that he had more faith in Fiona's ability to get out of bad situations. He knew Anya was a tough, fierce fighter. But the fact that she was a norm negated all of that. It would take little effort for Cora to kill Anya. Even if Anya somehow managed to free herself from her bindings, she was no match against the vampire.

"That's far enough," a female voice called down from the platform when they were about ten yards away.

He stared up at the two women on top of the airship loading dock, trying to gauge the situation. Even at this distance, he could see that there was something wrong with Anya. Instead of the rage or fear he would expect to see, her face was slack and expressionless. No, not expressionless, dazed. He couldn't see her eyes, but he instantly knew they were glassy and unfocused, the pupils dilated.

"Why isn't she moving? Why isn't she fighting that bitch?" Fiona's voice was shrill with fear and anger. "Anya could easily take that knife from her, vampire strength or not. Why isn't she?"

"She's drugged," he ground out.

"That skank," Fiona spat. "It makes sense that the only way she could keep Anya from killing her is to get her high. She probably bit her."

Jarrett didn't tell his friend that there was more than the endorphin producing enzymes in vampire saliva causing her sister's lethargy. He had a feeling that she'd been given a dose of whatever Python had been peddling at Wet Willy's. The same drug that had already killed two people. And Jarrett had no doubt that, despite the lack of evidence, Python was the drug supplier they'd been trying to catch.

The flickering firelight from the hot air balloon revealed a sickly pallor to Anya's skin that he knew Fiona couldn't see, and judging from her drooping shoulders and the way Cora's arm about her waist seemed to be the only thing holding her up, Jarret knew the situation was much worse than he'd first suspected. Her legs hung limply at a slightly odd angle. He couldn't be sure, but he suspected Cora broke them. If Anya weren't drugged right now, she would likely be in a great deal of pain.

Rage slammed through him, and the only thing that kept him from charging the tower was the fact that he could still see Anya's chest moving. As long as she was breathing, he had hope of getting her out of this alive.

"Cora, this is between you and me. Let Anya go," he raised his voice only slightly, knowing that even at this distance Cora could hear him even if he whispered.

"You aren't in charge here, Jarrett," she called down, raising her voice for effect and the benefit of Fiona's non-vampiric hearing. She placed the tip of the dagger beneath Anya's chin, pushing up so that her face lifted into the moonlight. Jarrett didn't have to see it to know that a thin rivulet of blood trickled out of Anya's pierced skin and down the knife blade.

Fiona howled and started for the tower's stairs, but Jarrett grabbed her arm, jerking her back. She screamed and fought against him as he held her tight.

"Fiona, stop it!" he ordered. "You can't go after her. She will slit Anya's throat before you hit the bottom step."

High above them, Cora cackled. "Listen to him, girlie," she taunted, bringing the knife to her lips and running her tongue over the blade. "Mmm. It would be a shame to waste all this delicious blood."

Fiona kicked against Jarrett's hold. "I'll show you just how girlie I am when I shove my boot up your ass," she screamed.

Jarrett tightened his grip. "Fiona, shut up," he growled in her ear. "Please, let me talk to Cora. I will get Anya out of this, I promise."

Fiona stilled, letting her body relax in his hold. He warily let go.

She turned on him, growling. "I'll let you do the talking, for now. But if my sister doesn't make it, neither will you."

"Knife in heart. I remember," he said, and briefly flashed back to the conversation they'd had almost two weeks ago, before Anya had become more important to him than any other human ever had been. Two weeks before he'd put her life in peril. He should have turned and walked out of the bar, and her life, that night.

"Are you two finished gossiping down there?" Cora called. "I'd like to get on with this, I've got places to be, people to slaughter."

Out of the corner of his eye, Jarrett saw Fiona's fists

clench, but she remained quiet.

He took a step forward and yelled, "What do you want Cora? Tell me what you want me to do and I'll do it. Just let Anya go."

"I can't do that. You see, I want you to suffer like you made me suffer. That means taking from you what you took from me. Your love, your world." She ran the back of the knife up and down Anya's throat as if in a caress.

"Well then you've got the wrong woman," Jarrett lied. "You know there isn't ever going to be anyone that means that much to me. Not after you."

"Liar. You've been with her every night this week," Cora screeched.

"She's just a fuck, Cora. That's all." He was surprised he didn't choke on the words. "Killing her will do nothing to me, but it will piss off the Nash City Blades. She has family in high places."

"It's true," Fiona called up. "She's my sister and the Commander of Nash City considers her his niece. Let her go now, and we won't hunt you down and cut you into a million tiny pieces."

"Ha, the Nash City Commander. How is old Sam? Or should I say, how are you, Sam? I know you're lurking out there somewhere." Cora lifted her voice so that it rang out in the night.

Sam stepped from behind a building about twenty

yards away. "I'm here, Cora. What they say is true. Let the girl go, and you will go unchallenged. As a matter of fact, I have the authority to guarantee you immunity from all Blade pursuit."

"You and I both know you only have that power for this crime, no other. But it doesn't matter, my old friend. This girl is the answer to all I've yearned for over the past eight months. Jarrett Campbell's destruction." She opened the small door in the side of the hot air balloon's basket and stepped inside, dragging Anya with her.

"Cora, I'm telling you, she means nothing to me. No more than any other innocent person. Take me, and leave her here." Jarrett was careful to keep his voice steady, pleading, but not desperate.

Cora let out a screech. "You can lie to me all you want, Jarrett, but I know the truth. I've watched you this past week. I've seen the way you look at her. She is your entire world, and I'm going to take her away from you, just like you took my world, my love, my heart."

She turned and nodded to Python, who cut the tether and triggered the crystal-heating element in the center of the basket. The balloon began to slowly drift away from the platform.

Fiona burst into a sprint towards a nearby platform. Jarrett knew it was with the intention of taking the balloon and pursuing Cora, but something told him it was futile. Something kept him still, his eyes glued to Cora and Anya in the basket.

Cora palmed the knife, putting her fingers to her mouth and blew a kiss to him. A loud buzzing started in his ears and the entire world went into slow-motion as she grasped the knife, put the blade to Anya's throat, and pulled it across in one long slicing motion. Blood bloomed from the wound. Then, as if she were a rag doll, Cora lifted Anya and tossed her over the side of the basket.

Jarrett's feet started moving before he even knew he meant to. He streaked across the lot, jumping the remaining distance. He caught Anya in his arms, but the momentum of her fall took them both to the ground. He pulled her close and rolled so that his body took the brunt of the contact. He immediately, and as gently as possible, rolled her off him and onto her back.

Through the buzzing in his brain, he could hear chaos around him. Fiona ran towards him, her feet pounding in rhythm to her screams. "No, no, no, no."

Sam, still on the other side of the lot screamed into a scry-crystal. "Shoot to kill. Take that balloon down. And where are the damned medics? Get the med-mages here now!"

Boots pounded the ground, arrows shrieked through the air, voices yelled orders, but as Fiona dropped to her knees next to Anya's body, his world narrowed to only the three of them.

He pulled his shirt off and pressed it over Anya's throat, but the blood soaked through instantly. "Help me. Put pressure on the wound."

Fiona's hands covered his, but it didn't help. The blood was oozing out, and Anya was getting paler by the second. Her breath was so faint he could barely hear it.

"It's too much blood. The med-mages aren't going to make it in time," he said nearly choking on the words.

"Campbell, don't you fucking let her die," Fiona screamed at him, her voice harsh and ragged.

He could save Anya, but she would hate him. He could save her, but lose her forever. He could save her and condemn her to a life of loneliness, of watching everyone she ever loved die. But the alternative was losing her and living an eternity knowing he could have saved her.

He looked up at Fiona through dry, burning eyes. "It's too much blood. The only way…"

"Do it," She choked out, blood and tears streaking her face.

Wordlessly, his eyes never leaving Fiona's, Jarrett grabbed the dagger from his waist and in one swift motion, slit his own wrist.

At first the blood oozed out slowly. Then it began to stream down his arm, mingling with Anya's. He pulled his shirt away from her neck and lowered his arm so the blood flowed directly into her wound. It wasn't doing anything. It wasn't working fast enough, she was too weak.

"I need more blood," he said, holding his other wrist out to Fiona, the dagger in his palm. "Cut this one."

"Jarrett, that's dangerous. If you lose too much blood..." she said, hesitating.

"Do it," he repeated, using her earlier words and tone.

She grasped the blade and slid it across his wrist.

He held that wrist over Anya's mouth, hoping that drinking the blood would help strengthen her so the virus would have time to take hold and heal her.

"Come on, Ginger. Don't you go out like this. You fight, you hard-headed little thing. You fight like a demon. I know you can do it," he choked the words out, fear and blood loss slurring his speech.

After what seemed like hours, but could have only been seconds, he heard Fiona let out a whoop. He looked up to see Anya's wrist between her fingers.

"It's working Jarrett," she said, her voice jubilant. "Her heart is still beating. It's slow, and weak, but it's beating. And look, the wound is closing."

He looked down and saw she was right. Part of the gash on Anya's neck was knit together and looked like it was several days old, instead of minutes. It was a start, but she was so weak. He had to keep giving her blood until the entire wound closed. It was the only way to insure the virus had taken hold.

"Jarrett," Fiona's voice sounded far away. "That's enough, the healers are here. They'll take care of her. You saved her. She's going to be okay."

"No, I have to make sure." His throat was dry, and his head ached, but he had to make sure Anya survived. If she didn't get enough of his blood into her body through the wound, she would still die.

"Damn it! Sam, help me!"

Jarrett heard Fiona whisper to Sam, and he wondered why she was talking so softly. Then he felt strong hands pulling him back and pushing him onto the ground. He tried to fight them, tried to get back to Anya, but they overpowered him.

"Damn it, boy, be still." Now Sam was whispering. "He's lost a lot of blood."

"Put his wrist in his mouth. The saliva will help seal the wound and stop the blood flow," someone else said, from far away.

"Anya," he gasped. "Anya."

"She's right here, Jarrett. She's going to be okay." He felt someone put something in his hand, and he knew it was Anya's hand. It was limp, but warm. She was warm, she was alive. She may hate him forever for what he'd done to her, the fate he'd forced upon her to make sure she survived, but she would live and that was all that mattered.

He let the darkness hovering around the edges of his vision take over.

About the Author

June is a geek girl, fat chick, and unrepentant romantic. She writes full time and is both independently and traditionally published. She also works part time running her greeting card company.

When not working, June can be found making jewelry, reading, cooking, or watching geeky movies with her husband and snuggling with her 6...YES 6, furbabies. Notice cleaning wasn't listed...

Acknowledgements

The acknowledgments section is always one of the hardest parts of a book for me to write. I wouldn't be able to write anything without the amazing people in my life, but I'm always afraid I'll miss someone and hurt their feelings. I think I'll keep it simple this time.

First, I want to thank everyone who read Voodoo Moon. On the days when writing is super hard, I think about the reviews and the messages I received asking for more stories about the Moon sisters. It keeps me going.

Second I want to send a special shout out to two members of my street team, Amy Stogner and Kristy Hamilton. Amy spent her summer helping me with promotional duties so I had time to write. Kristy read every single chapter of Immortal Moon as it was written, giving feedback to help make it stronger. I am so lucky to have such wonderful people on my team.

I also want to thank my sister, Tammy, because without having known and loved her for these past thirty plus years, I'd never be able to write the beautiful relationship between the Moon sisters.

No acknowledgments page would be complete without an "I Love Your Guts" to my #1 Bish, Sherry. She encourages me, deals with my crazy, and pulls me back into the land of the sane when I've gone over the edge.

And last, but never least, my husband Steve. He is my answer to life, the universe, and everything.

www.ingramcontent.com/pod-product-compliance
Ingram Content Group UK Ltd.
Pitfield, Milton Keynes, MK11 3LW, UK
UKHW041305180426
11947UKWH00009B/694